RADIOLAND

by Bob Pondillo

RADIOLAND

by Bob Pondillo

© 2025 Robert J. Pondillo

ISBN 979-8-9938411-0-6

Table of Contents

Early Praise for Radioland

"★ ★ ★ ★ ★" Funny, sad, and all the feels in between. *Radioland* takes us on a heartfelt and most unexpected inward journey."—David H. Lawrence XVII, actor, entrepreneur, audiobook narrator.

"A new voice has burst upon the scene. *Radioland*, screenwriter Pondillo's first foray into novelized fiction, is easygoing, heartbreaking storytelling. A joy to read. Unforgettable."— FC, from the Internet.

"It's hard to describe the profound impact radio had on society in the 1960s, especially on younger listeners, but Bob Pondillo did it, and does it just about better than anyone. Radioland is a remarkable story that needed to be told."— Mike Olszewski, radio/TV/newspaper reporter, non-fiction book author, and historian.

"You have a winner here! Every one of us who survived the radio wars of the 1960's and 70's will read this novel as a shared, lived experience. Reading *Radioland* I had a broadcasting flashback on just about every page. Here's a novel for readers who enjoy stories like Jean Sheperd's 'A Christmas Story' or the films of Cameron Crowe, but with a richer and deeper exploration of the cost of hanging on to one's illusions."—Eric Braun, former radio/TV news reporter/director, media consultant/Frank N. Magid Associates, VP International Television for the Associated Press, London.

"*Radioland* is a vivid, witty, and warm fable for anyone who remembers hiding a transistor radio under their pillow and listening into the night. It earns tears and plumbs philosophical depth to the end."—Mary Hood Hart, retired educator and freelance writer.

"Great job! For anyone who ever slept with a radio under their pillow, *Radioland* captures a boy's fascination with and passion for the business. Also, his disillusionment as he matures and sees behind the scenes."—Jon Belmont, 50+ years in the broadcast business, CKLW 20/20 News, CHUM, 1010/WINS/New York, ABC Radio News, and the Associated Press.

"How can a child understand truth when he's surrounded by falsehood? It takes him nearly his entire life to understand, but only by running the gauntlet of *Radioland*, does he gloriously learn. A haunting story."—NP, reader from the Internet.

"Bob Pondillo (whom I knew as "The Real Bob James" when he deejayed on 1220/WGAR in Cleveland) does an excellent job on recreating a time when radio was a dream for a young boy (as it was for me) and when the medium was well done. Radioland was quite moving for me and highly recommended."—Dan Haber, Top 40 jock, CFTR, Toronto, Ontario; producer/editor at CityTV, Canada.

"*Radioland* is a moving story about life, acceptance, and healing. Really enjoyed it!"—JP from the Internet.
"It's a little story, about a little boy, who, from his little bed, wrestles with life's biggest questions. *Radioland* is eye-opening. It shakes the ground."—TF, an Audible listener.

"*Radioland* tells the tale of how a little boy growing up in postwar Cleveland learned many hard and valuable life lessons, not only by listening to his favorite (albeit mind-sick) deejay but from directly participating in the marvel that, back then, was KYW Cleveland. Great stuff!"

—Professor Richard Klein, Cleveland State University (ret.)

"If you changed radio stations when the record started playing to hear what another radio station's air personality was going to do next, you're a 'radio guy.' *Radioland* is a novel about how Top 40 radio stations in the 1950s-1970s captured the imaginations of Baby Boomers with their portable transistor radios always at their side. It also tells the hard truth about the business side of radio's "show business." This second Golden Age of radio is the world I grew up in, and Radioland wonderfully brought it all back to life; sweet, funny memories tinged with a few drops of necessary tears. Loved it!" —Dick Taylor, retired broadcast professor,

School of Broadcasting & Journalism, WKU, blogger, lifelong radio guy.

Dedication

My deepest gratitude goes to Edie, my sweet wife, first reader, truest critic, and lifelong companion, whose insight and love shape every word I write.

Introduction by Dick Taylor —

First off, I loved this book; please excuse the bromide, but "I couldn't put it down"—and this novel isn't industry booster-ism wrapped in pretty prose. There's some tough stuff within these pages. Bottom line: it's about one little boy's negotiation with life and truth—messy ideas with which, sooner or later during our days on this planet, we all must deal. The novel just happens to be set in the equally messy world of radio.

This story takes place during the rise of 1960s AM radio, but a true understanding of the sting of life can bubble up from any setting: on a football field or a baseball diamond, in business or a hospital emergency room. With a different backdrop by a different author, this book could have easily been called Football-Land or Baseball-Land, Business-Land, or Hospital-Land; yet, each different story would ultimately arrive at the same conclusion. The setting may be different, but the ending will always be touchingly human. These stories we tell ourselves in the limited context of our own lived experiences—from childhood to our adult years—can only make sense once we step back and arrange the pieces in a sequential, rational order with clear cause and effect. Only then do we make them "mean" something. Only then do we move from confusion to clarity. As does the novel's twelve-year-old main character, Tommy Bianco, in Radioland.

When I was a kid, about Tommy's age, I changed radio stations when the record started playing to hear what another radio station's wacky air personality was going to do next. Why? I think that, back then, I was searching for something more, but just didn't realize it. Perhaps it was a way to shape my yet-to-bloom sense of self. Sure, I knew all of the epoch's great tunes and loved them, but Top 40 radio stations from the 1950s-1970s captured my imagination in another very personal and mind-blowing way. This was a magical time, fraught with uncertainty not unlike today with our smartphones and the emergence of AI. But we Boomers had the precursor of them all: the transistor radio. In October 1954 the Regency TR-1, came on the market just in time for the holiday season. This tiny, new, mass-produced technology meant we could now carry portable, tubeless radios with us at all times. That innovation changed our lives as much as silicon chips have transformed today's youth culture. *Radioland* wonderfully brought this seminal memory back to life for me.

Radioland also tells the hard truth about the business side of radio's "showbiz." It's about a fleeting chapter in AM broadcasting before all the commercial clutter and the rise of FM and so much damn noise that prompted future generations to move on and be captivated by an even more personal medium: the Internet.

The second Golden Age of radio is the world I grew up in. Now, looking in life's rearview mirror, it was also an eye-blink in time. Radio's Golden Age happened shortly after the birth of commercial broadcasting in the 1920s. It was a time of fifteen and thirty-minute radio programs with stars like Jack Benny, Bob Hope, George Burns and Gracie Allen.

Radio's second Golden Age, with television coming on strong, is when the medium had to reinvent itself. Thus, format radio was born with stations focusing on talk, news, or narrowly focused music programming. Smart operators quickly understood that the rock 'n' roll music of our youth, along with the portable transistor, would make AM a hot commodity for advertisers wishing to cash in on our burgeoning generation, and that gave birth to the Top 40 format—only 40 songs repeated constantly all day long. It was a counter intuitive idea, but it actually worked.

Radioland is a story about this exciting, chaotic period in broadcast history. It's about how a fatally flawed deejay, playing a stack of 45-rpm records, along with jingles, sound effects, and a wild imagination, would capture the heart and mind of one innocent little boy. It was a time when local on-air "personalities" frequently became more popular than TV and movie stars, often even more popular than the records they played. But no matter how much fun a deejay made it appear, inside the radio station, management was in constant pursuit of the almighty dollar—and before "best practices" were established—programmers might try any questionable tactic to keep capricious teens tuned in. It was (and still is) a simple equation: more listening meant higher ratings, and high ratings could increase commercial ad rates and a station's revenue. It also meant advertisers held tremendous editorial sway over what was broadcast.

As for me suggesting that Bob Pondillo, the author of this work, might like to turn his story into a novel? Well, that's true. I'd read an early draft of his screenplay from which he crafted this work and absolutely loved it, but the movie industry moves slowly on such matters. Nonetheless, I sensed this story really needed to be told now, somehow, someway. So, yes, the result is this book. But happily, other than writing this foreword, that's where my literary involvement ends, and our generous friendship continues. I sure am happy that Bob took me up on the idea. I think you may be, too.

—Dick Taylor, CRMC/CDMC

Retired Broadcast Professor, The School of Broadcasting
& Journalism, WKU
Blogger—Volunteer Air Personality—Lifelong Radio
Guy

November 2025

Preface —

This work is a "novelized memoir"—a combo meal of fiction, history, and semi-autobiography. It's based on radio stations and deejays I listened to as a kid and some actual events recalled from my more than thirty years of on-air performance in terrestrial radio/TV broadcasting. I've chosen to tell it both in the shadowed and composite repackaging of the voices who lived it and in the persona of a much older guy who "remembers" it.

My intention was to create a story told in a relaxed prose and patois. A work that reads like a one-sided conversation over coffee between friends. A recollection of a blink in time that might also hold some compelling literary value.

What you're about to read, then, is a twizzlered, embellished musing on the past—but presents a fairly authentic, albeit fictionalized, recollection of a life in radio, from which a reader might draw a few simple universal truths. I hope you'll find it an often funny, frequently sad, but mostly a rewarding experience—sort of like life.

I chose to use the word "manikin" in the story, not "mannequin" like the dummies you see modeling clothes in a department store. The Manikin conjured here is a dark, uncanny fiend—a life-sized, human-like body that moves in shadows. A "Thing" that is at once there and not there. A specter that flits from the corner of an eye, then vanishes.

Finally, *Radioland* was originally written as a full-length motion picture screenplay. I've adapted its story into this novel to make the telling richer and more complete. It's for you to decide—should the movie ever get made and you see it—if the book was better. Either way, let me know what you think: pondillo@gmail.com.

Prologue —

Once upon a time… a little boy fell in love with his own imagination—he just didn't know it at the time.

He was tricked by a beguiling seductress who carried him to strange heights of illusion, where real life blurred with dreams.

Did he fly to Narnia, or tumble into Middle-earth? Was it Azeroth or the Land of Oz? Well, no. Not exactly. But since this is my memory, and the boy is me, let's just call it Radioland.

In the 1960s, there were Radiolands all over America. Mine happened to be in Cleveland, Ohio—a good enough place for a twelve-year-old kid to grow up, so long as my reality was filtered through something called AM radio.

Now, I was no electrical engineer, but I knew AM meant amplitude modulation and that it lived on a spectrum of invisible light, with its frequencies measured in wavelengths from 530 to 1700 kilohertz. These days, hardly anyone listens to AM anymore. A stray newscast, a ballgame, the cock-sure voice of some delusional preacher—that's all that remains.

But back then, from my tiny transistor radio and its swirling nighttime heterodyne of squawks and squeals, I heard my imagined world.

ONE — Life in Radioland

"Everything that enchants…deceives."—Plato

I'm pretty sure I fell under the spell of Radioland under the cover of my nighttime blanket tent. It was sometime after Christmas 1965.

I was twelve, almost thirteen, and it was cold and snowy, the price paid for living near the fourth largest of the Great Lakes, Erie—and its attendant "lake effect" weather. So, it was just me, my blanket fort, my transistor radio, and my sweet little dog, Walter.

Over the air, a jingle choir crooned a picture-perfect postcard of my town. It was "Radio 11's"/KYW Cleveland Love Song, and it ran like a movie in my mind.

"Oh, Cleveland, Ohio… we want you to know… " The jingle sang.

When I'd hear it, I could "see" two romantics holding hands near the reflecting pool at Erieview Tower Plaza. It was summer again, and when the lovers kissed, fountains gushed skyward to a zoomed-out wide shot—typical of TV and movie-style productions of the time. It was as if the city was bathed in Technicolor and filmed in Panavision.

"We love the looks of the sun as it shines on your windows… "

Yet, real Clevelanders know that any winter sun is rare and that "window shine" is most likely a half-inch of frost—inside and out. At that moment, I bet'cha someone on "America's North Coast" (Cleveland's fancy name) coughed into ice-caked mittens, as a plow folded a ton of snow like bad origami.

"We love how the raindrops sparkle in your trees and the way your city sounds on our pretty melodies… " The jinglers jingled.

That's exactly the moment a man's shovel cracked in two, and he pinwheeled backward into a frozen drift—his middle finger punching up through a pile of fluff with a resigned, "FUCK ME!"

"We love to ride to the top of the Terminal Tower... And gaze down at you below by the hour… " The singers harmonized.

Yet, in my kid's cartoon mind, gazing down from the tower's fifty-second floor, I watched lake winds blow Public Square stoplights until they leaned like drunks leaving a bar. And I imagined a man's ears freeze solid and fall off, his face glaciated into a permanent Munch Scream.

"The time on the Shoreway thrills us through and through… " The song went on.

Nope. I heard drivers stuck in place inbound, locked bumper to bumper, spitting profanities that would make Jesus cry.

"Oh, Cleveland, Ohio… KYW wants the world to know we're in love with you…"

Was it love, or a calculated lie? Neither really. It was all just benign showbiz, and while I can't be certain, I'd like to think I subconsciously understood that but didn't care. Most likely, I didn't yet realize that, thanks to radio, the Cleveland I loved had a second city standing right on top of it, a fully constructed alter-ethos, a soundtrack version that sang of freezing rain as sparkle and winter as a Christmas card. Plato sure was right: lies do indeed enchant. That was Radioland, a place that broadcast a cunning and perfect "city of sound" layered over the actual one. And even if I "kind of" knew about the disconnect, I chose to live in the fantasy. Why? Well, I suppose Baby Boomer kids were just different back then.

There was a special holiness to a single 50,000-kilowatt stick on a great lake. KYW Radio, at 1100 kilocycles, was a federally licensed "clear channel" station. At bedtime, the signal bounced off the ionosphere and skipped to central Canada, Midwest, northward nearly to the pole, before heading down toward the Gulf. That charged layer of atmosphere took Cleveland's voice and trampolined it back, bigger and prouder. AM after dark could make an immigrant-filled steel town feel like the center of the world. Wow is a technical term when you grow up with that kind of power blasting down your block.

Inside the dim, sagging walls of my blanket tent with the transistor glowing, I listened, inching the dial past 770/WABC, New York, to 800/CKLW, Detroit/Windsor, to 890/WLS and 1000/WCFL, both in Chicago, as if I was scanning the constellations. It was

23

something we radio geeks called "DXing"—distant transmissions—and we collected them like baseball cards. Walter, my mutt, ears cocked at the high-pitched tuning squeals, dropped his head and sighed with puzzled dignity. Yep, my blanket bunker was about to usher in the "Greatest Show on Earth," and Walt was the other nonpaying customer.

Then—snap!—the world shifted, and I was back at my favorite, and for me, the best station in Radioland.

A slow, sweet, brassy jingle smacked the night airwaves from 1100/KYW's deejay booth. Over the music came "Swingin' Dicky Peppers" purring into the microphone.

"Mm, yeah, baby," his voice dripped with goofy mock seduction. "Time to cuddle up with your hubba-hubba man... " Dicky bobbed and weaved his voice in and around any pauses in the sultry melody, interacting and reacting to rests in the vocals.

"When the sun turns out its light..." The singers jingled.

"Oh, make that room dark, honey!" Dicky encouraged between breaths in the lyrics.

"…and calls it a night... "

"Ooo. "Nighttime's the right time, girl!"

"When the moon begins to glisten… "

And Dicky, unable to resist, sang his own serenade into the groove—"…with sweaty bodies!"

The singers, oblivious, carried on: "…it's the perfect time to listen to—"

"Wait. Perfect time to wha?" Dicky broke character, catching his own absurdity.

"... K-Y-W…"

"Guess that'll have to do!"

"…in Cleveland, Ohio… "

Triumphant, he cued Chick, his sidekick in studio control, who answered by slipping in the opening strains of the Beach Boys' "In My Room" like a satin sheet.

"It's the World's Greatest Trumpet Player," Dicky crowed over the record's intro, "on K-Y, with tonight's spotlight dance, baby. Oooh, the Boys of Beach, spincerely yours, with a lay-d'yah's choice-ahhh!"

The music swelled. In my little fort, Walter cocked his head again, and my grateful heart sank into the glow.

Swingin' Dicky Peppers was thirty-two and maniacally funny. Dicky was the kind of deejay who interrupted the world as if on a mission from God. Most announcers had deep, sonorous voices. Not Dicky's. His was loud, higher-pitched, kind of squeaky in its own way, and brash, but full of heart. He kissed the mic, gave a sour honk on his trumpet, and then unleashed a Sonovox, a metallic, robotic HUBBA-HUBBA that sounded like something between a laugh and a catcall.

A Sonovox doesn't whisper, y'see. It screams through you. The way it works is gloriously simple and weird: you feed a tone or instrument into two transducers that, when pressed to your throat, allow the vibrations to ride on your larynx. Your mouth shapes vowels and consonants while the instrument supplies the music—the Sonovox literally borrows your voice, like a ventriloquist's trick. Dicky used it to make horns talk like men and women sound like steel guitars! It was ear-catching, wacky, and it made me laugh until I (almost) wet my pajamas.

I fell asleep that night in a place the real world could never enter. And convinced myself I'd found a home.

Morning didn't so much arrive at our house as break in. In the mid-1960s, winter in Cleveland etched frosty ferns on the inside of windowpanes, and the air tasted like icy iron filings.

I was in rare form that morning, struttin' downstairs like a pint-sized Arthur Godfrey in socks, ready to deejay myself into glory.

Our console stereo—mahogany, hulking, devout—sat like an altar against the wall. On its turntable, a 33⅓ album sat ready, spinning beneath a taped nickel on top of the tonearm. This particular LP cover promised transfiguration. Its title: "You Be a Disc Jockey." It was a comedy-minus-one kind of thing; after the jingle played, I'd jump into the dead spaces to practice my deejay patter until my voice felt unshakably "boss." Well, at least to me.

"You Be a Disc Jockey" was my twice-daily lesson and a game of donut jingles—little musical holes edged in to insert my voice—like Dicky did. It was practice, and I was an eager student.

"Tell me the station I'm listening to— " the singers jingled.

I cupped a hand to my ear, puffed out my chest, and let it rip.

"Thisss   is   Double-You-Bee-Dee-JAY, everrrybody!" I bellowed in my best puke-announcing voice.

"How 'bout tellin' the time with me?— " the jinglers asked all sugary and perky.

"It's a fabulous three-fifteen A-YEM, guys and gals!" I answered. It wasn't. I was practicing, okay?

From the kitchen came the slow burn of my Mom's stare. She stood there—thirty-something, hip cocked, butter knife in hand like a weapon of maternal judgment, her foot tapping in irritation on the linoleum.

Meanwhile, Carmel, my sister—nine-years-old going on a prosecuting attorney—kneeled backward on a chair, peeked over a Superman comic with a crooked smirk she'd perfected. Milk dribbled down her chin into cereal like she was auditioning for Slob of the Year, her eyes rolling so far back she could see her own brain.

"THOMAS, NOW! COME EAT!" Mom hollered, her voice sharp.

From the living room, courtesy of the worn-out album, my "backup singers" kicked in.

"And what's the weather gonna be?" The jingle singers pressed on mercilessly.

Carmel groaned from her perch, shaking her head as if I was beyond redemption.

"Cleveland, Oh-HO-HO weather calls for snow on the roof, and a high in the low nineties..." I sang out, mixing clown with crooner like the world depended on it.

"THOMAS! NOW!" Mom barked, ratcheting the threat level to Defcon One.

I sagged theatrically, raising my hands in mock surrender. "Sorry, kids, no more today, cuz yours truly, Tommy Bee, has gotta go eat."

In the kitchen, Carmel shook her head, not believing that we shared the same DNA.

But I wasn't done, not yet. From the living room, I jabbed the air and tossed my closing line over the heads of my imaginary studio audience: "But, I'll see yeh tomorrow with a lot more grrreat snowstorms then!"

With a flourish, I swiped the tonearm across the spinning record, giving it a cheap scratch, worthy of any real deejay's horror.

Carmel slapped her cheek and muttered, just loud enough for her comic book to hear: "What an ASShole."

I bounded into the kitchen still bopping to my private soundtrack. Without breaking rhythm, I grabbed a spoon from the counter, raised it like a golden microphone, and puke-announced once more, unstoppable, untouchable, and—to everyone else in the house—unbearable.

"Yes, yes, yes, Momma! It's your very own, Tommy Bee! Buzzin' the top off the ol' pop crop!" Then I popped my cheek with a finger. I did my own sound effects back then.

Mom, frazzled from keeping the household upright, grabbed back the spoon before I could do more damage. "Uh-uh!" she snapped, shoving a plate of toast into my hands and pointing me to the table. "Sit!"

I slumped across the kitchen in protest, grumbling the whole way. But I looked back at her, smiled, and in my head, I heard the jingle singers again:

"Sweet Adelaide! Our household's bride. She's crabby now, but always on his side! It's Tommy's, Mom! It's sweet, sweet A-de-laide!"

Carmel was kneeling on her chair, wagging her butt at me like the brat she was, and ready to unleash her usual morning skunk spray.

"CarMEL! DON'T! YOU DARE!" Mom roared.

She didn't listen, of course. She flicked a Corn Pop at me with incredible accuracy. And sure enough, in my mind's ear, her jingle chimed in:

"That's Carmel! Carmel! Nine years old, bratty and brassy! And if you smelt it, it's cuz she dealt it! Cuz she's a little gassy! CAR-MEL!"

Right on cue, Carmel put me in her Dutch oven. She did her own sound effects, too.

"Aw, man! MAAAH! She did it again!" I yelled, waving the air.

"CarMEL! Not at the table!" Mom scolded.

"Snitch," Carmel shot back.

"Dope," I countered.

I stared down at my toast, sulking, then brightened, picked up a fork, and went back to my routine. "Hey everybody," I announced into the tines. "It's Wo-Wo-Wonder Bread! Helps build strong bodies twelve (twelve, twelve) ways (ways, ways)!" Yep, did the echoes, too.

"MAHHHM!" Carmel whined.

Mom raised her butter knife like a saber. "HEY! I said no more talkin' in the silverware!"

"I hate that stupid voice," Carmel muttered.

"It's called announcing, idiot!" I shot back.

"TOMMY!" Mom warned.

"But, MAAAH!" I whined.

"It creeps me out!" Carmel piled on.

"CarMEL!" Mom flared again.

The whole mishigas grew until my Dad's voice boomed from the doorway, a one-man gavel slamming order into chaos.

"YO!"

For a moment, it felt like the Dragnet theme filled the kitchen. Dum-de-dum-dum! And in my head, it had! Another jingle kicked in, too:

"Vin Bianco! Scariest man on the planet! It's Tommy's DAD, Vin Bianco! Uh-oh!"

Dad stood there, thirty-eight, worn down from a double shift at the mill, a cigarette clamped between his teeth. He squinted at us, and with the weight of the world on his shoulders, said the only word that mattered:

"EDGY…"

The room went dead quiet.

"…CATION!"

You could feel the syllables slap the walls. He jabbed his smoke in my direction like a conductor stabbing a downbeat. "That's the only way out for yuns two dumb jamokes."

Carmel stopped smiling and sat up straight. Walter dropped his head between his paws and whimpered. Even ol' Walt knew today's morning sermon would soon begin.

"I never wanna see youse go to work wit a lunch bucket under your arm, y'hear? And no more lippin' off to your mother!" He set his dented lunchbox on the counter and kissed Mom on the cheek without lowering his filtered Kool. "SIT!" Dad commanded, and the chairs obeyed.

If you want to know why I remember that morning so clearly, it's because of the way the word education left his mouth. I think Dad thought that if he said it loud and often enough, the idea might shove whatever snarling future he feared for us back down the stairs.

Dad's name was Vincent, but at home, Mom called him "your father" when she was protecting him from us, and "Vinny" when she was protecting us from him. He had only made it to the tenth grade before life provided a different curriculum. So he preached school like a Catholic convert. He didn't know how to teach softly. He knew how to bang on metal until it became useful. And to him, being useful was essential.

We ate in a silence that wasn't really silent. You learned to hear the unsaid in our house. Mom's fork tapping her plate exactly once before she set it down (nerves), Carmel's heels swinging and knocking the chair rung in threes (defiance), and Dad's breath coming a hair faster than normal (anger misfiled as concern). My mouth made the toast disappear while my head counted music beats. I wanted to tell Dad I was involved in a kind of "edgy-cation." I was doing homework, studying how the deejays on KYW bent time around their voices, but the older me, the one who would grow up to be a doctor, already knew he wasn't listening for that kind of answer. He was listening for our promise not to become him.

And that was that. Dad never let a storm in our kitchen pass without dragging it back to the same point: school, education, books.

"Hey, I don't care if you hate me for that," he said, "but always respect your mother, y' hear me?"

He wasn't subtle about it either—he wanted me to know that whatever dreams I had about radio, snowstorms, and microphones meant nothing if I didn't have a diploma in my hand. At the time, I thought he was just being a buzzkill. Years later, I realized academics were really my only lifeline out... and up. Yeah, there were only three of us in my extended family:

me, Carmel, and my cousin Richard (he became a lawyer), who escaped the hard labor life of Cleveland. My other cousins and their kids still work in, or have recently retired from, decades of backbreaking work at the mills, factories, and foundries of Northeastern Ohio. I've always admired them, too. I could have never done that.

Dad put out his cigarette in his empty coffee mug, stood, and the room clicked back into morning. He side-eyed me once, with a look that said, Don't end up like me, and I love you in a grammar he didn't know how to speak.

When he went to the bedroom to peel off the mill, Mom touched my wrist. "He's grumpy when he's tired," she said softly, and there was a whole life in what she said. Let him rest. Let him not be the person he has to be all night. Let him not worry that he's already failed you.

Carmel's eyes darted toward me and narrowed, but not in mockery this time. For one heartbeat, we were on the same team: two siblings trying to make sense of a dead-on-his-feet, working-class father. Then she smirked, flicked a new Sugar Pop at me, and wiggled her rear in another celebratory butt bomb. Mom rolled her eyes. "CarMEL! NOT at the table," she said, tapping the butter knife on the counter. I laughed. Carmel giggled. Yeah, my sis knew a good hot-boxed toot worked better on me than kindness did.

As we walked toward our daily destiny, I held my transistor close to my ear. Carmel, in a conspiratorial whisper, nudged me back to reality and said, "Y'know, I saw Ghoulardi blow up a dead mouse with a firecracker right on TV! It was outta sight, man!" It was also gross, childish, and wrong. And yes, Ernie Anderson, who played the Cool Ghoul and scary movie host for years on Channel Eight got in trouble with sponsors, but we kids ate it up.

In fact, every time Ghoulardi said "Parma," where we lived at the time, he'd drop polka music under the line as if the whole neighborhood was the punchline. We, being proud Italians, thought that was a riot, of course. And dumb Polish jokes were everywhere back then. I know, "Ew," right? But they were. Even our own Catholic Church still did minstrel shows for fundraisers in the 1960s! I mean, actual, full-on, blackfaced, racist minstrel shows in a freakin' church! Can't say we were very "enlightened" back then. Pop culture of the era, with its outdated ideologies, flew under the radar of civil consciousness and stuck to us like Gorilla Glue.

At the corner stop, the snow looked like stale frosting. The yellow bus rounded the block with the cheerful resignation of municipal duty, doors folding open with a sigh. A few girls, with ponytails and Kleenex carefully tucked in training bras, waved at me. I waved back, shy but mostly disinterested, like a diplomat from a small, secret nation.

Mr. Toomey piloted the morning bus. He was fifty-something, hang-dog face like a used leather baseball glove. I bopped up the steps, my radio blaring the funniest morning team on KYW Radio, Specs Howard and Harry Martin.

"HEY!" Mr. Toomey barked, "Nuh-uh! I run a quiet bus here, boy."

"But Specs and Hare is on the air," I blurted. "The kids'll love 'em!"

Mr. Toomey stared, his eyes narrowing. "Put it away! Now!" He extended his hand and growled, "Or gimme!"

I snapped off the transistor and shoved the contraband in my pocket. "Aw, cripes! I really love those two guys."

"Love?" he snorted. "How's that matter?" His hand found my sleeve, tugging me closer, and with the saddest eyes I've ever seen, said, "You're chasin' the wind, boy."

At twelve, the sentence was off-putting. Later, I would recognize it was part of a parable from Ecclesiastes, a book from the Hebrew Bible. But the way Mr. Toomey looked when he said it stunned me.

"Um, sure. "Okay," I said, and took off down the aisle to claim an open seat by the window, sinking low like a fugitive. Out came the transistor—my cheap, plastic holy grail. I jammed in the earpiece, clicked the dial, and—zzzzzt!—static melted into Radioland. I was safe in my fortress of sound.

Then came a telltale wheeze and a thud beside me.

It was Alvy Hevel. Round as a meatball, nose forever congested, lenses thick enough to spot Sputnik, and my best bud, sidekick, and shadow. The kid was welded to me like a Siamese twin in corduroy pants.

And right then—bam!—the jingle singers in my brain tore open the curtain like a morning zoo crew.

"It's Al-vy! Alvy Hevel! Short and round, Cleveland's pride, Tommy's best pal —stuck to his side! It's AL-VY!"

"Hey, what'cha doin' down there, Tommy?" he asked.

"Alvy!" I said, sliding up, brightening, holding out the earpiece like a priest with the Host.

Alvy sat—same grade but fourteen, older than me because he'd been held back a year. He was small for his age, glasses forever sliding down his nose, hair in his eyes, with a steady discharge of shiny sniff. That day, he smelled of Vicks and pencil shavings, and we were two of the nerdiest radio wannabes on the planet.

"Dig on this, man! It's so boss," I said.

We leaned temple to temple so he could hear the day's most hilarious episodic bit Specs and Hare ever did. "Here," I said, and pushed the earpiece toward him. "There's a new Congo Curt on KY!"

Alvy listened, blinked, and pushed up his glasses. "But, um, no... see, nothin's ever new up in the sky, Tom-bo."

"Huh?"

"Wait," he squinted hard, processing a thought. "No, um, it's 'nothin's ever new...' um...'Under the sun.' That's it. Cuz, cuz..." Alvy recited his lesson slowly: "'One generation passeth away, and another generation cometh'... and, and, and 'there is no remembrance of former things." He nodded proudly.

Wow. Ecclesiastes again? I thought that had to be a cosmic coincidence, never considering that the universe was already trying to tell me something. But at the moment, I surmised that Alvy was practicing for his upcoming bar mitzvah.

The adult in me wants to stop the tape here and warn you: four years later, that funny, earnest little boy, my closest pal, Alvis Amos Hevel, would die in Vietnam's ugly Tet Offensive. Eighteen. Yeah. Regretfully, we had a stupid, childish fight long before he shipped out, and I never apologized. The heartbreaking news, when it came, silenced our entire block in a way no snowstorm ever could. But on the bus that day, he was my sniffly (albeit horny) buddy who always thought girls saw him as a real charmer. He wasn't.

Me? No, I wasn't into girls back then. When girls waved. I ducked. I wasn't into sports, either. Even Top 40 music itself—though it soaked into me—wasn't the point. My fantasy was radio itself. She… err, it was my only object of affection. What possessed me was the deejays' voices: all men—very few women were on the air back then—the patriarchy, y'know? Anyway, these jocks could surf a sixteen-second record intro and kiss the vocal on the downbeat. Guys who could lie to your ears and make millions feel the truth, a lot like the Bible. Outrageous personalities who made me laugh until I hurt. Why? Maybe it's because a voice doesn't judge your shoes, or clothes, or your father's calloused hands. A voice could be a person and a magic spell at the same time.

I remember Alvy saying it as softly as paper rustles: "There's nothing new under the sun." But what he said reminded me of the stories my Mom used to tell about all those past radio giants.

And then—poof!—live action gave way to another goofy cartoon daydream in my head.

Three framed photographs—George Burns and Gracie Allen, Jack Benny, Bing Crosby—bobbed into view, each standing stiff before an ancient NBC microphone. Their mouths, crudely hinged like dime-store ventriloquist dummies, with cuts in their chins that flapped open and shut.

Up there in the attic of my brain, I did all the voices myself.

George Burns cracked: "Say g'night, Gracie!" And she returned a nasal, ditsy, "G'night!"

Jack Benny drawled, "Oh, Rochester, y'see…!" And Bing Crosby, crooner turned delinquent, sang with syrupy mockery: "Buh, buh, buh… blow job!"

The photos, now scandalized, plummeted from their perches. CRASH! BOOM! SMASH!—each landing in a cartoon garbage can.

"Yup. All gone!" I sighed, then smiled and thought, all replaced by something new and to me, waaay better under the sun!

Cue the animated cartoon JUKE JOINT in my head, neon lights flashing, music pumping, absurdity triumphant.

Legend has it that Top 40 didn't grow out of a memo; it crawled out of a jukebox. Picture Joe's Juke Joint somewhere in Texas or Oklahoma: the floor sticky with beer, a neon sign frying the smoke an egg-yolk yellow, a glass-topped jukebox the size of a refrigerator purring with a carousel of forty 45s.

The story goes that two South/Central station owners (and salesguys)—Todd and Gordy—who fancied themselves radio programmers sat in the corner, watching and listening. They kept track of songs patrons played on the jukebox without looking like they were tallying.

A happy cowboy fed the box a nickel. The arm lifted, and an Ames Brothers disc dropped: "Rag Mop," from 1950. Needle down. The room nodded; the song played. Then the happy cowboy fed in another nickel and chose the same record. Then, another nickel. And played the exact tune again. Todd scratched a hash mark; Gordy drew diagonals. Suddenly, a mean cowpoke got mad, shoved his way over, a bottle smashed—and a hockey game broke out! The jukebox, faithful as ever, just kept playing. And when the hook hit, "R-a-g-g--M-o-p-p! Ragmop!" even in mid-melee, the room obeyed: voices chimed in, boots tapped, heads bobbed. Todd and Gordy looked at their pencil marks, not the brawl, and grinned like two guys naming a new baby. "We'll call it...Top Forty!" They yelled together, delighted with the idea that they could sell repetition on the air. With network radio dying and TV coming on strong, this idea could be peddled! And popular, repetitive music was Radioland's newest salesman.

Is that how it really happened? I mean, factual like a police report? Maybe not. But radio never needed affidavits; it needed myths and deejays that sold records. The lesson stuck: figure out what music people can't stop playing and feed it back with jingles in between commercial breaks. Radio became a giant promotional wheel, and the song's hook was the crank.

After school that day, back in the kitchen, Mom slid a glass of milk toward me and didn't mention the C+ in math I'd tried to hide. "You gonna try out for that morning announcement thing?" she asked.

"Aw, Mom. They only pick eighth graders."

"You could be an eighth-grader enough, if you try," she said, without planning it.

I put the milk down and cleared my throat. "In school news today," I intoned, "the cafeteria is proud to announce the return of... meatloaf pizza!"

She clapped twice, softly. It felt like church. Mom was always on my side. She made me believe I could do anything.

After supper, I spun "You Be a Disc Jockey" again, hitting post after post like a boy who believed timing record intros could move mountains. Carmel watched and muttered under her breath, "Freakin' dweeb." But it was too late for me. The bug had bitten, and I was poisoned, but in a good way, or so I thought.

That night, Dicky's voice crawled back into my blanket tent, where I slept with Walter. Every time I laughed at Dicky's jokes and funny asides, Walter would awaken and cock his head with a look that said, "What the hell, man!? I'm sleepin' here!"

"Good evening, my children of the night," Dicky said with a Bela Lugosi flourish, his trumpet honking an off-key laugh.

I fell asleep to that sound—and reviewed all the many insignificant things that made up my young life: Dad's frequent sermons, the spoon mic, Mr. Toomey's sad tug on my sleeve, Alvy's bar mitzvah practice. And I thought I knew then what I didn't yet: the rooms inside Radioland would sometimes be lies, sometimes be dark, and sometimes be unseen terrors in empty chairs that could scare the shit out of you. I didn't know about the pills or the books by Camus that would arrive soon enough. All I knew was that listening to radio felt like home.

In the morning, Dad would split EDGY-CATION in two again, not to change my mind, but because the ritual calmed his future fears for me and Carmel. The steadiness my Mom and Dad provided was a real blessing to a twelve-year-old like me. They gave me everything a kid absolutely needed: the house was warm, solid, and predictable, always a refuge of love. That was enough to anchor me on my strange, liminal journey toward Radioland. The business was built on the constantly shifting sands of commerce and public taste.

TWO — The Wizard's Curtain

"The truth is rarely pure and never simple." — Oscar
Wilde

So one time, I couldn't tell you exactly when, KYW Radio was doing a Meet Your Favorite Deejay thing, and the whole city was invited! Well, you sure didn't have to ask me and Alvy twice! This was our chance to meet Swingin' Dicky Peppers in person!

That day, I remember the bus brakes. That first iron scream when the driver stomps the pedal, and it sounds like John Coltrane hitting a high note. That's how our Saturday began—the CTS sighed to a halt at East Sixth, doors yawn-hissing, diesel breath in our faces. Cleveland in winter pinched cheeks like my Aunt Margie, slush was the color of old gray pennies, and Alvy and I were full-blown radioheads.

"This is it," I said. I stared at the KYW radio and television building's side doors. These were holy doors to me—a veil to part as you entered a kingdom where voices are bigger than people.

Alvy jittered beside me—sniff, tug, zip, push glasses up, sniff again. "C'mon, Tommy! We're gonna be late! What if all the good-lookin' babes already got in?"

That was my best friend in one sentence: the world was a mixer, and all the cool girls were inside it.

I handed Alvy a torn-in-half piece of my last stick of Wrigley's, and we were ready.

We crossed the street and walked straight into the smell: Aqua Net, Brylcreem, and the churn of a hundred teenagers trying on what they thought was adulthood for an afternoon. A sandwich board yelled in CAPS. Marketing Top 40 radio in the '60s meant you had to shout to be friendly:

KYW RADIO V.I.P. ROOM!

Starring Cleveland's Own: THE SECRETS

…and KY's Nighttime Favorite, Swingin' Dicky Peppers!

"Groovy," I said, which was Ohio for I'm about to freakin' pass out.

"Hey, Tommy. You think Dicky Peppers is tall?" Alvy asked, dead serious.

"Why?"

"Because I'm afraid of tall people."

"How come?"

"I dunno. What if he… licks my head?"

"What? Alvy, that's stupid. Besides, we're in seventh grade."

"Right." He nodded gravely. "Tall, then."

We drifted across the sidewalk and stepped in front of a tired Volkswagen Beetle. Maybe a '58? Inside, a guy hunched over a paperback in the driver's seat, holding the book close to his eyes, oblivious to the growing crowd nearby.

We didn't clock that it was Dicky at first. I'd seen photos of him in the paper, and this fella had no halo, but I remembered a rule my Dad told me: when you finally meet a person who lives in the drapes of your head, they generally don't match the carpet. Or something to that effect. Anyway, Dad thought it was funny.

So, this "Dicky" seemed taller than his voice but somehow heavier than his body. His mouth moved as if he was tasting the sentences he read. Later, I'd learn the book was Albert Camus' Create Dangerously. It's about how artists need to embrace risk and produce work that challenges social norms and injustices. At twelve, I thought Camus was a fancy shampoo.

Inside the Slug Bug, something happened that I'd only understand later and still flashes in my mind. Dicky glanced at his watch, flinched like it stung him, and jerked upright. Through the back window, in the rearview, I could've sworn—I did swear—a Faceless Black Manikin sat, like a dead passenger. No eyes. No mouth. Just a polished absence. Dicky spun, recoiled, breathing hard, and the Thing was gone, the way a nightmare slams the door when you wake up. He swallowed, agitated, dropped his book, grabbed his battered trumpet like a defensive weapon, glanced at the back seat once more—still empty—then kicked the door open with his shoulder as if the car itself had to be escaped. Yep, it was Dicky, alright.

"Tom-bo," Alvy whispered, "What's 'a matter?"

"Nothin'," I said, which is precisely what you say when you think you'd just seen the worst thing you can't name.

We joined the line. Smiling ushers with skinny ties pressed KYW V.I.P. buttons into our fists like sacraments. A girl group, The Secrets, lip-synced their only charted song, piped in from somewhere. The reason for featuring The Secrets was that they were one-hit wonders and from Cleveland. As I looked around, mouth agape, I saw teenage girls in frosted lipstick smoking with practiced boredom, and the boys smelled of their fathers' aftershaves. And, no shit, everyone was chewing gum. Go figure. Gum and orthodontics were fixtures of '60s teenagers.

For the V.I.P. party, KYW Radio had commandeered one of the television studios and shoved the TV cameras, sets, and bleachers of The Mike Douglas Show to a corner. My Mom watched that show, and I remember seeing it one summer—the time the Beatles were Douglas' guests after their earlier "invasion" on Ed Sullivan.

Then Radioland swallowed us—glass doors, the pop of heated air, the smooth linoleum, the walls stamped with KYW logos and giant cardboard 45s. Yeah, the place was a "boss groove!"

The room itself—converted to be the Apollo—buzzed like a transformer. A makeshift riser at one end, The Secrets still lip-syncing their only hit in front of a sea of parkas and ponytails. The dim space with brightly spinning TV spotlights was nobody's friend; they'd bleached us all the same color: pale and nervous… with pimples.

We were only a few steps in when a man in a rumpled suit appeared at my shoulder. Balding, glasses, with the eyes of a hustler. A cigarette hung off his lip like it paid rent.

"Yuns two here to see Swingin' Dicky Peppers!?" He barked, pointing at me as if I'd ordered the pastrami special. He shoved his business card at me: Menachem Reuven Keagels/KYW Sales. "Here you go!" Then he pivoted, jabbing a thumb toward backstage, then back at us.

"Youse wanna meet him… in person?" he asked.

"Dicky! In PERSON?" My mouth said, and my knees answered, Let me just die now?

"Hell, yeah!" Alvy said, simultaneously checking the odds of kissing three separate girls in the next hour.

The man smiled with half of his face. "Good. First, pass these out to everyone. Then... I'll see what I can do."

He slapped a stack of glossy coupons into my hands, then into Alvy's. "Free giveaways, kids—Big Boy shakes and some zit cream crap. Don't eat the ice cream." He winked.

"So listen, yuns two call me Merk, all right? How yeh doin'?" he said, sticking out his hand as an afterthought. "Just Merk, get me?" He pointed to his card, "That there's my government name, but that ain't what we use 'round here."

If you want to picture Merk, imagine a man who has lived four separate lives in one county: foreman for a tire company, hawker of used high school saxophones, a stint at an amusement park concession stand, and now—against his own expectations—selling radio time. Ken Apati (we'll get to him) had pulled Merk out of sales to "watch Dicky," which sounded like babysitting until you realized it was exactly babysitting. Merk didn't call himself a producer; he called himself a handler. He herded talent like cats, and Dicky was his only cat. "Chop-chop," Merk said, clapping his hands once, loud enough to make my stomach remember. "Move 'em, kids. I want everyone in here holdin' 'em things. You too, Shorty."

He'd already nicknamed Alvy. Of course, he had.

We became paperboys in the temple, shoving coupons into clammy hands, our fingers smelling of last-minute printer's ink. Merk's one-sided negotiation was clear in the way street trades always are: do this, and payment would not be in money. It would be in entry. Merk's promise—a tiny, off-the-record contract scribbled in the air that said, in effect: Help me grease this crowd, and I'll walk you through any freakin' door you want.

"Hiya, hiya, don't be shy! Come on in, kids!" He barked to the queue behind us, his cigarette orbiting without ash. "Meet a star and get you an autograph better'n a report card. And free shakes! Comes with a free napkin, too. Tell your mom it's dairy. Dairy's good."

"Dairy's good," Alvy repeated solemnly to a girl with a beehive, shoving her a coupon because sometimes echoing a salesman makes you feel like one.

We were elbow-deep in teenage humanity when I saw Him: Dicky, peeking from the wings like a fox checking a henhouse. I moved closer and watched, trying not to be seen. He cradled the trumpet at his belly. His eyes were bright, maybe too bright—fever or ambition, I couldn't tell. He pressed a hand to his temple, winced, then peered out at the crowd the way you look at scary waves from the lip of the East Ninth Street Pier. And I surprised myself for feeling protective of him.

Then, a hand in a black leather glove, wrist confident, landed on Dicky's shoulder. Dicky flinched as if he'd been caught by the CIA.

"Yeah," said the glove's owner, sliding up sunglasses that weren't strictly necessary indoors. "Welcome to big-time radio, huh? This is how it works now, man."

That was Ken Apati. Thirty-something. Hair that didn't move unless he commanded it. He was the Program Director, which meant he controlled everything, including the weather inside the building. Ken spoke in imperatives and dressed in italics—shades, a Nehru jacket, and Beatle boots, trying hard to come off as "just one of the hip kids"—and a little too cool for school.

"I don't... I can't do it, Ken. Not today," Dicky said. "No way."

Here's the thing with Dicky's voice: most jocks sounded like they'd smoked a bassoon. Dicky's was high and sharp, brash and boyish, like a squeezed accordion on two legs. Even scared, I sensed he was interrupting the show for its own good.

"C'mon, Dick. "Again with the attitude?" Ken said intensely, but without raising his voice. "Don't be difficult. Just do your act. They'll love you. They already love you."

"Look, I'm a studio jock," Dicky whispered. "I don't know what these kids want."

Ken smiled like a Vegas blackjack dealer. "Wha? You think they do? They're teenagers. They got no fuckin' clue what they want. So we tell 'em, this is what they want." He tapped the stage with his foot. "What's the damn problem now?"

Dicky stared off the riser like he was standing at the edge of the Red Bull Diving Cliffs. "I, I, I didn't sleep. Can't eat. I feel… sick, man."

Ken's face softened just a hair, then re-hardened into company policy. He reached inside his jacket and poked a pocket flask into Dicky's ribs. "Here. Go ahead."

"No. I can't. I, I'm not supposed to… "

Ken took a hit. "It helps," he said, which is what every pusher says, whether they're selling booze, ratings, or a story you need to keep an employee functionally vertical.

Somewhere in my chest, an alarm sounded that I didn't understand.

Dicky's fingers shook. He took the flask, not drinking yet, just letting it cool in his palm. He glanced toward the back hallway—escape route, bathroom, closet, all roads lead to anywhere else.

"Let's go, Dicky-boy," Ken said, tugging his sleeve. "C'mon."

"NO! Will ya STOP!" It came out too loud. He closed his eyes and swallowed. "Just… gimme a minute, please… "

Ken studied him with a squint.

"Cover me," Dicky said finally, "Just this time. Please, man."

Ken took another slow pull from the flask and placed it back in Dicky's hand. "Fine," he said. "One time, Dick. Once!" He adjusted his collar. "It's showtime, baby."

Ken stepped out to the mic with a smile he'd rehearsed in mirrors, and the room loved him on principle. "Let's hear it for Cleveland's own, The Secrets! With their smash hit on K-Y's Sound Eleven Survey!" The girls bowed. The boys whistled. Cleveland congratulated itself for living here.

Backstage, Dicky fished in his pocket for a small red pill, the kind kids in chemistry class had only heard about. His face did the math. He popped it, chased it with the flask, and clutched his trumpet.

He leaned against the wall, his eyes beginning to unfocus. And then—you know those tones you used to hear when a TV station went off the air at 2 a.m.? Imagine that note busting into your skull and making itself at home. I think that sound built an invisible room around him. He clapped both hands to his ears. And where a minute ago there'd been a vacant backstage, there stood the Faceless Black Manikin from the VW again—but closer this time, almost above him, a presence like pressure. It was as if those non-existent walls took a step in, then got closer still, squeezing Dicky.

Dicky extended his arms, sweaty palms out, trying to hold back the crushing fear. The Thing stared at him without eyes. Malevolent, grasping, it seemed to want to absorb Dicky's essence. It crept closer, hunched lower, and moved in for the kill.

Then—bang!—the backstage door burst open, slamming concrete, and the Manikin was gone; silence faded back to crowd noise.

Merk led the way, carrying a coffee the size of a small bucket. Alvy and I trailed behind, our pockets light with coupons but heavy with purpose.

"There he is, boys!" Merk said, already performing. "The boss groover himself. Jus' like I promised."

Dicky wiped both cheeks fast. He turned around as if the last few seconds were a dream. He smiled—too wide—and shot to his feet.

"Dick," Merk said, "meet two'a yer biggest fans."

Dicky pointed at us with an index finger like a magic wand. "STUNNER!" He shouted the way he said hello to anything that delighted him, snagged the coffee from Merk, and started to gulp.

I just shone as I watched him. Then Dicky's jingle popped into my mind:

"He's the funniest guy you'll ever know! The wackiest guy from head to toe! Most popular guy on radio! It's Swingin' Dicky Peppers, on K-Y-W in Cleveland, Ohio! Swing, Dicky, swing!"

As Dicky slurped Merk's coffee, he mis-aimed the swallow, and with the last brown mouthful, sprayed a glistening arc onto Merk's face.

"It's CRAP!" Dicky announced, eyes ping-ponging.

"My hero!" I laughed out of startle; then Alvy laughed because laughter is contagious. Merk laughed, too, because he was a professional and had a handkerchief.

"Dicky, ya nut," Merk said, dabbing his cheeks. "Say hi to two great kids. This is—ah, tell 'im."

"I'm Tommy," I said.

"I'm very short," Alvy added, on brand.

Dicky beeped a few sour notes on the trumpet—ba-da-DOO!—and bent in for the shake like a man who made eye contact for a living. His hand was warm and shook with the current of adrenaline-fueled anxiety.

And there he is, said the narrator in my head (which was me), I'm gonna be just like him! It was the precise moment a boy made himself a vow without words.

On stage, Ken milked the crowd. "Up next, the deejay y'all been waiting for—the Guru of Horn! Your hubba-hubba man himself! K-Y's most bodacious nighttime jock ever—Swingin'! Dicky! PEPPERS!"

The room exploded in cheers, chanting, "Hubba-hubba!" Dicky tucked the trumpet under his arm, rolled his shoulders, and walked into the spotlight.

Well, he didn't simply enter. He detonated! Jump—split—spin—knee slide—trumpet blare. It was show business crossbred with a sick, nervous system. He stomped the mic stand, then leaned into patter like a drummer leans into a fill.

"Turn into peanut butter!" He yelled over and over, and the kids yelled it back, faster and faster, like a game that made as much sense as you needed if you're only twelve.

"Hubba-hubba! Whoo!" Sweat. Eyes big as silver coins. If the stage had a speed limit, Dicky meant for it to lose its license.

Not much later came the part that made it real to me—the autograph table—where our god sat. Dicky scrawled SWINGIN' DICKY PEPPERS in loops and apostrophes across 8x10 glossies while we, still deputized by Merk, slid more coupons into hands as they passed. Then, a woman-girl stepped up—Sally, I'd learn later—radiant in the way small towns produce: perfect makeup, hair coiffed like a movie star, high school ring on a chain, oversized football jacket (not hers). She smiled. Dicky looked up and said, "Stun-NER!" giving her his full attention.

Ivy, Sally's wingwoman, stood behind her, less radiant and therefore, to me, more interesting. Frumpy-cool in a way that felt chosen, with a Polaroid camera at her chest like a tin heart. She raised it, snapped, whirr-chirrrp, and a square coughed from the black mouth of the machine, a secret that needed sixty seconds to tell.

"Hey, honey, can we get us a picture too?" Alvy said to Ivy, affecting Sinatra through a head cold.

"I guess." Ivy rolled her eyes without too much malice and lifted the camera again.

"Keen-o!" Alvy said, elbowing me. "Tommy! Get over here!"

We leaned in near Dicky, whose attention slid back to Sally's nubile beauty the way iron finds a magnet. Ivy's camera chirped. The black sleeve spat the shot. She shook it and waved it in the air to dry and work its magic.

"Wow! Thanks a lot!" I said, because gratitude is my native language. Then our handler arrived.

"Back to work, yuns two," Merk said, materializing at our elbows, herding. "C'mon, c'mon, move the line. Move, move, MOVE!"

The line rushed by, and we didn't have a chance to grab the photo Ivy made. Damn! Maybe next time, if there's a next time. And slowly, that afternoon swelled, then thinned, as all afternoons do.

Hours later, the teen crowd was gone, and the V.I.P. Room exhaled me and Alvy onto the sidewalk. I was almost thirteen, but felt I had aged by proximity. The wind off Lake Erie seemed to bite less, too. Alvy held up a wad of remaining coupons and grinned at his haul.

"Look'a this, man! Free chocolate shakes till we freakin' die," he said.

"And," I said, palming Merk's business card—a rectangle of promise—"we got this!" Yep. Merk liked us enough to ask if we would like to help out on Dicky's show. He told us to drop by the station next Monday! What a mind-blower!

"Us?! Workin' in real radio! You're shittin' me!" said Alvy.

"No, man, that's what he said!"

We hadn't taken five steps before we saw Ivy leaning against the building, camera case at her hip, puffing a smoke, and waiting in teenage boredom. Alvy eyed her and decided to make his move.

"Ooo, yeah, baby! My lay-d'yah," he announced to the street, patting his chest and strutting into a future that would not claim him. "Well, hellooo, there... sweet thing."

Alvy opened with the kind of small talk that immediately dies on an untrained tongue. "So, ah, I see you still enjoy the instant photo-TOG-raphy, hm?"

"Mmm, so?" she said, the most efficient critique in English. Then the uncomfortable pause.

"Um. Who? Me? Radio," Alvy said, as if anyone had asked. "Yeah," he sniffed like Barney Fife, "I'm… workin' in it."

"Really? You know the Beatles?" she asked, a test that weeded boys faster than algebra.

"The Bea—? Oh, sss-sure. We… we've t-talked. Once. On the… on the phone. It was a b, b, bad connection."

"Alvy," I rushed in with the save, tugging his sleeve, "Sorry. We gotta go."

He waved me off and whispered, "Ix-nay, Ommy-tay. I'm havin' a real moment here." He fished a handful of coupons out of his pocket for Ivy. "Um, say you like shakes?"

Before Ivy could say, I'm not really into short boys who talk like a-holes, Alvy glanced past her shoulder at the building. "So, hey, where's your friend?"

Back inside the now-empty KYW-TV studio where they'd held the party, on the other side of a thin closet door with no lock, Dicky and Sally were engaged in, let's say, a collaborative sport that we as kids did not yet have the vocabulary to narrate. Some adult secrets you learn to intuit. Stuff you might learn from movies, a Sears catalog, or from whispers in gym class showers. Kids understand that two people behind closed doors were "conducting sexy business" that was totally none of ours. Anyway, the door clicked shut just as Merk rounded the corner, his jaw tightening as if this had become routine for him and Dicky.

Back outside, the bus rumbled to the corner. I yanked Alvy by the sleeve in the ancient choreography of boys who rescue each other from themselves.

"Come on, man, or we'll miss it, I said, and we started our scamper. Just then, Ivy called out.

"Hey, kid!"

Alvy turned.

"Other one," she said, which was both an insult and an inventory. She held out the finished Polaroid she'd taken earlier. The chemicals had done its alchemy, and there we were in the shot—Tommy, Alvis, and, behind us, Dicky in a blur that was prophetic: two dopes grinning and their idol caught mid-motion behind them.

Even then, Dicky looked ready to retreat to an errant closet for some touchy-feely... or more.

"Whoa," I said, accepting the photo. "Thanks a million!" and meant it with my whole heart. "Really? This is the best day of my entire life." And I meant it.

Ivy smirked. "You'll think different later," her face said, because some people have already learned that the cost of a dream is listed in very small print.

Back inside the studio and down the hall, that closet door opened. Sally emerged first, cheeks flushed, tugging her skirt, and eyes straight ahead. Merk stepped in, not blocking, just intercepting. He held out two tens like a man offering cab fare.

"Hey. Whatever happened in there... didn't," he winked.

"You're damn right it didn't," Sally said, and snatched the bills. She left with the posture of a girl who understood her reputation. She'd just heard an invitation, saw an opportunity, and found it fully acceptable.

Dicky followed a beat later, his face downshifted from morose to shame. He tucked in his shirt, zipped his pants, and spotted Merk.

Merk didn't say a thing. He didn't have to. He lit a cigarette off the butt of the one that had almost ended. He just glared at Dicky and exhaled in a way that said, I was hired to keep you on the rails, man, and they gave me a fuckin' roller coaster!

That night back in my blanket bunker, the transistor glowing and furry ol' Walter snoring into my knee, Dicky returned to his on-air show, the only place he'd never failed me. I imagined what it was like to be in there with him. I'd know soon enough, thanks to Merk, but instead, I tried to conjure every detail. Just how did all those little pieces of live radio get stuck together and produced in front of the whole world with no net to catch a disaster? Here's where visualization and my actual memory get crossed up and a bit fuzzy. So let me explain it like this:

Chick, Dicky's studio control board-op, clicked the talkback. I could hear him in the studio through my imagination.

"Comin' back in ten," Chick's filtered voice said. Somewhere on a cart machine, a commercial chewed its last second.

"I'll tag, then jingle into music," Dicky said. I could hear his grin.

Chick hesitated. "You sure about this tune, man?" he asked, because the board-op is the last adult in any room.

"Full responsibility," Dicky said, tapping his chest.

He hit the tag clean—"Available now at Halle's eighth-floor record department downtown!"—and Chick punched the jingle.

"It's another K-Y-W—encore! Encore!" the singers sang, and the goosebumps on my arms sang back up.

Chick readied to release a slip-cued 45 rpm with two fingers, pointed to the studio clock: 10:12 and 16 seconds, and counted Dicky in. Dicky hit the post like he was born inside the second hand.

"Ten-twenty-two, at K-Y in Cleavage!" Yes, Dicky deliberately told the wrong time and did, in fact, say "Cleavage," both causing the studio phones to light up. "Here's a hit that happened! Our No-No of the Night! Must be eighteen to listen! KINGSMEN!"

He dropped "Louie, Louie."

I laughed out loud under the blanket. Not Louie, Louie! Every kid knew it was "banned" for dirty lyrics that no one could actually hear. Really! The words were "obscene" and not "protected" under the law! Dicky had threaded the needle: play the rumor people can't stop believing, it's safer than playing the truth. All over town, teenagers sang a story they didn't know.

I laughed so hard under that blanket that Walter groaned and rolled over, smacking me in the ribs with his bony paw. Didn't matter. I couldn't stop. "Ha! Not Louie, Louie!" I crowed, tapping the rhythm onto Walt's soft belly as if it was a set of conga drums. My furry little pal bared his teeth, licked my hand, and sneezed, but I was off and running.

See, every kid in Cleveland knew the song had been banned. The story went that the lyrics were so filthy that the Catholic Church and the FBI had joined forces to protect our delicate ears. Picture it: J. Edgar

Hoover, in a lovely cocktail dress but his mascara a hot mess, squints into a reel-to-reel, slowing the tape down like a monk parsing holy scripture. "Did he just say, 'Fuck her again?' he'd whisper. As if national security depended on teenage hormones.

But that was the point: you couldn't actually hear the words. The lead singer—Jack Ely—mush-mouth-mumbled through a fog of garage-band distortion, like he had marbles stuffed in his cheeks. Pure nonsense syllables. And nonsense, ladies and gentlemen, is the mother of obscenity. Our imaginations did all the heavy lifting.

At the local A&W drive-in, the air smelled of frying onions and thick root beer syrup in frozen frosty mugs. Carhops in bright skirts skated between rows of Fords and souped-up Pontiacs. Radios blared the forbidden hymn, rattling out of tinny dash speakers. You could hear the mugs fizzing as kids banged the beat on car roofs. The boys wore their varsity jackets like armor; the girls twirled ponytails and tried to act unimpressed.

Behind Parma High's stadium, an anthropology class turned primal. A football game thundered in the background—the field announcer yammering into the winter night—but nobody cared. The real action was under the bleachers, where two teenagers, operating on pure lizard brain, mashed lips, pawed sweaters, and explored each other's belt buckles with sweaty, trembling hands. It was an extracurricular biology assignment, live and in color, and they were doing homework! The transistor radio squawked, "Louie, Louie" beside them, its beat matching the awkward rhythm of their various sexed-up discoveries. Then—like divine commentary—the end-zone scoreboard flickered on:

SCORE!

That was no accident. The universe has a sense of humor!

As for the Jets and Sharks' West Side Story version, you only had to glance into a chopped-down convertible idling near the grimy, not-yet-gentrified Flats of Cleveland on the Cuyahoga. Four greasers—slick Brylcreemed hair, drinking Iron City beers, Marlboros dangling—pounded the dashboard, belting out their own X-rated interpretation:

"Every night at ten, I [indecipherable] her again…"

It didn't matter; they couldn't make out the words. They filled the blank with sheer gusto, howling it into the night. The missing lyric was a Rorschach blot. Your brain drew whatever smut it wanted, and you swore that's what you heard.

And presiding over this whole carnival of testosterone, grease, and rumor? Swingin' Dicky Peppers, the Pied Piper of KYW Cleveland. He spun the record without apology, winked at the gossip, and kept just enough distance to be untouchable. That was his genius. He played the rumor, not the truth. Safer. Smarter. And a hell of a lot more fun.

Dicky knew what we half-believed and gave us plausible deniability wrapped in three chords and a microphone turned to mush.

Yeah, Dicky got away with everything.

And how could a teenager not love this freakin' guy?

The next morning at home, I decided to premiere a private floor show called "Make My Parents Love Radio." I had moxie with my toast. I staged it in the kitchen because every Midwestern teen-dream tests out its act in front of a stove. Or, didn't you know that?

At our Formica table, Mom stirred her instant coffee, Dad shook his head, and peered over Carmel's shoulder as she drew mustaches on a Superman comic. Me? I had an announcement. The biggest, I thought, of my twelve-year-old life.

"Mom, Dad," I said, chest puffed. "I have some very, very important news to, to… um, speak. "Please, if you will, take a seat, Father."

Dad scowled with a raised eyebrow at the odd behavior, then cautiously eased into a chair beside Mom. I sat across from them, holding Walter, my confused dog, as a prop.

"No kiddin', guys," I said. "I mean, THIS is big."

Mom leaned in. "Ooo! What?! Tell us!"

"Dad, Mom, get ready. You too, Carm!"

Carmel wiggled her rear, ready to blast her signature dishonorable discharge.

"CarMEL! Don't. You. Dare!" Mom commanded. "Go on, Tommy."

"Okay," I said, petting Walter for courage. "Um, well... I have decided that I, your son, Tommy Bianco—me!—I am going into... radio!"

Dad squinted. "What? To fix 'em?"

"No! To be on the air! Y' know, a deejay! To play music an' tell the time!"

Mom blinked. "But, Tommy, people already got record players and..."

"Clocks," Carmel added.

"...for that."

Dad's nostrils flared. "Deejay, my ass! You'll be a podiatrist like your Uncle Dub."

"Feet stink," Carmel muttered.

"HEY! They wash 'em before they touch 'em!" Dad barked, "Adelaide, help me here!"

Mom sighed. "Thomas, we thought you really wanted to be a doctor."

"No, Ma, I really don't. Aw, can't'cha see? If I'm on the radio, everyone will know me—and, and love me."

Dad shook his head. "Nah, nah. That's a sickness, kid."

Mom touched my hand. "Aw, don't you feel loved, Tommy?"

"'Course I do, Ma, but—"

"Radio, c'mon! Outside a, I dunno, Indians game, who in the hell listens to that goddamn noise?" said Dad.

That's when I shot up an index finger, Walter tucked tight under my arm. And then — boom! — Sarah Vaughan herself filled our little kitchen, Quincy Jones' brass section snapping in behind her.

I lip-synced every word, every syllable, like my life depended on it:

"Who listens to radio?…" I mouthed.

Suddenly, it wasn't our kitchen anymore.

I was at the beach, transistor clutched in one hand, Walter in the other, inner tube around my waist. Sand burned my toes as Sarah crooned, and I lipped the words:

"…that go where you go, medium called radio…"

Smash cut: traffic jam at dusk. Brylcreem shellacked into my hair, specs on, attache case wedged on the seat. Walter had both paws on the wheel, honking the horn like a maniac.

"…that's with you every night…"

The freeway oozed like hot lava.

"…through the long commuter fight…"

Walter barked, impatient as a cabbie.

Then morning light: I was back home, in a bathrobe, jar of orange jelly in hand. I dumped it on my toast, and Walter licked it clean.

"…and in the morning…"

I spread my arms like a Vegas headliner:

"…with your toast and marma-ladio!"

Cut back to our kitchen—Mom and Dad frozen, mouths agape—then whoosh, I was center stage in a white cyclorama, tuxedo tails, top hat, and cane twirling.

"Who listens to radio…"

Colored banners dropped behind me in perfect time.

"…no matter if it's summer, winter, spring, or fall…"

Mom's wide eyes blinked. Dad's, too.

Back to me, selling it big, Sarah's voice soaring:

"…Who listens to ray-hey-hey-hey-hey-dio?…"

On cue, a map of the U.S. lit up, states flipping red like dominoes until the letters spelled it out in lightning: A-M RADIO!

And I shouted the kicker, arms wide:

"…Only 150-million… 150-million people, that's all!"

Walter barked on the downbeat.

Then. Silence. Mom and Dad stared. Carmel, slack-jawed, froze in mid-mustache draw. Showbiz over.

Dad slammed his fist. "BullSHIT! Them radio jagoffs play that goddamn sex, devil music! Look! Look here!"

He lunged for the black-and-white TV on its rolling cart. The screen fizzed, then exploded with images: teenagers writhing, shrieking, caught in the delirium of rock and roll.

The voice-over announcer thundered, "Teenage savages go wild in a juvenile jungle of lust and lawlessness, all because of pagan rock and roll music!"

A preacher jabbed a finger at the camera. "It is a contributing factor to the juvenile delinquency of today!"

The v/o announcer's stern voice warned, "That two-beat pattern is the music brought to the United States of America by the communist conspiracy to corrupt our teenagers!"

Then came the cherry on top: a fat, bald "expert" radioman clutching a brittle 78 rpm. He smashed it against his turntable like Moses shattering the tablets.

"Rock and roll has got to go," he crowed. "And go it does!" He grinned like a man who'd just saved Western civilization.

Dad folded his arms, satisfied. "There. You see!"

And me? I just stared, dumbfounded, while the narrator in my head cut in: Riiight. But thank you, Jesus—Top 40 deejays and rock 'n' roll were here to stay!

Dad pushed angrily away from the table and stomped off. A tired man with a lunch pail's worth of fear. His life was telling him one thing, and his son was singing another. He was trying to warn us of the real future he'd lived: in the heat and sweat, his overseers grasping with greed. It was an image that haunted him. No, I just didn't get it then.

After that, we ate. Just the three of us. In silence. The fork tapped once. Carmel kicked the chair rung three times. The dog breathed like a small metronome. The room filled with the unsaid. And in the quiet, I heard yesterday's chant again: "Turn into peanut butter!" It sounded stupid now, but beautiful too. Sometimes the holy and the dumb wear exactly the same suit.

After breakfast, I went to my room and pulled out the Polaroid. Have you ever held an artifact, and it feels like heat in your hand? There we were: me, Alvy, our radio life about to happen; and behind us, Dicky—turned half away, eyes already on a teenage high school doll who mesmerized him. It was only a relic, yes. But also a warning label you only learn after it's torn.

I thought about Merk's half-wink and hustle. The way he orbited Dicky, a fire extinguisher hired by Ken to keep Dicky from self-immolating. I thought about Ken's cool control as rationed compassion, requiring results. I thought about the Faceless Black Manikin in the VW Beetle, sitting there reflecting a secret malady.

Radioland didn't really transform anything. It wrapped reality in a jingle and timed it to the top of the hour.

Don't get me wrong: I still believed. Belief is a jacket you keep wearing even after you notice a rip in the sleeve. I was twelve. The glass doors had opened for me at that KYW V.I.P. party, and the room had been real. The girls were "ginch," the music "fab gear," and my idol actually existed. Dicky had shaken my hand. Merk had paid us in entrance to Radioland. Ken had sold a show to hundreds of teenagers and one boy who would be counting beats in his head for the next sixty years.

Radioland's "jingle-Cleveland" was beautiful, so I chose to live there, even as the lake punched a stoplight sideways and the broken-shovel man's middle finger stabbed through a snowdrift like he was drowning.

That afternoon, Alvy came over to practice record intros. We timed our patter to hit the vocal, kissing it on the downbeat because that's how pros show affection. He sniffed between takes. "Hey, Tom-bo," he said. "You think Merk meant it? About workin' for Dicky? Like... for real?"

"Yeah," I said, staring at the ceiling like it contained the future diagrammed in pencil. "He meant it all right."

"How can you be sure?"

"Because he needs us," I said. "And… we can do the job."

That was a new feeling for me—that you could earn your way through a door by being useful. Not special. Useful. The world always opens for the useful, then bills you.

Some nights, even now, I think back to Dicky peering into that rearview mirror and seeing the Thing that didn't have a face but somehow looked exactly like him. On good nights, the Manikin stayed in the car. On bad nights, it followed Dicky into the deejay booth, keeping unwelcome company. I found out later that he tried to get better, to shake off the darkness. I know he did—I saw it firsthand. But the music still had to start on time because Chick was counting you in.

Back then, though? Back then, I was a boy with a spoon microphone and a Polaroid, and I'd just stepped through the looking glass.

If there's a moral here, it's this: the first time you see behind the Wizard's curtain, don't run. Look. Memorize the ropes, the pulleys, the man who keeps a flask for emergencies and calls it encouragement, the handler who laughs with coffee on his face, and the girl who takes pictures because she knows people lie.

Then go home. Crawl under your blanket. Let the voice tuck you in again. Fall asleep to the No-No of the Night and the silly chant that turns frozen peanut butter into something spreadable. In the morning, my father would split "education" into two syllables again, my mother would tap her fork once like a prayer, and I'd carry a tiny station ID inside my chest and whisper it to myself on the hour.

Three — The Pledge

"Every act of communication is, in some way, an act of translation." — Octavio Paz

The city bus lurched to the curb, engine wheezing, brakes screaming, and tires sloshing in downtown slush. Alvy and I tumbled out into the cold, a diesel cloud wrapping around us, the breath of Cleveland itself. I had Merk's business card pinched in my hand, edges softening from too much fondling. Only a few days ago, we'd been coupon-flinging paperboys, shilling Big Boy shakes and pimple cream, and today we were invited inside!

Inside! Not just some backstage pass. Not just a handshake. The actual KYW Radio studios. The shrine to our youth. The citadel!

We dashed across East Sixth, almost flattened by a noisy Chevy whose driver leaned on the horn with a personal vendetta against two kids on foot. Then we pressed ourselves against the thick plate glass of KYW, penitents at a cathedral window.

My breath fogged the glass, but through the cloud I saw everything. This wasn't a reception room—it was heaven with tasteful incandescent lights. Nirvana with a receptionist. For me, it was like witnessing the Big Bang.

Then, as if on cue, music rose and a jingle played in my mind: The KYW Cleveland Pledge.

"K-Y-W... K-Y-W..." the singers sang reverently.

Instinctively, my right hand went over my heart, my left cupped around my eye toward the lobby. The tears came uninvited, but I didn't care.

"Now we proudly pledge allegiance to the station that we love..." the jinglers and I piously sang.

Behind the desk hung a chrome-and-glass logo: "KYW AM/FM/TV, Group W." Beneath it, perched like a pinup girl in a business suit, was Rhonda. She couldn't have been more than twenty-four, hair sprayed into architectural compliance, blouse cut low in ways seventh-graders could only dream about. Cigarette dangling, magazine open, she barely looked up. To Alvy, she might as well have been Venus on the half shell. His eyebrows waggled like Groucho Marx in Duck Soup. Me? I just kept softly singing along, my voice cracking.

"To the friend that we depend on, we sing the praises of! K-Y-W… K-Y-W!"… I sang.

On the far wall hung clocks, lined up like soldiers: Cleveland, Chicago, Los Angeles, London. The world measured out in minutes, all of it somehow owned by this station. Even time had to check in with KYW.

Rhonda exhaled a plume of smoke, shrugged, and turned a magazine page.

"We'll be true to you forever… forever and a day. From our great hometown of Cleveland, wherever people play…"

Not angelic lyrics exactly, but close enough for a kid who thought he'd stumbled into God's kingdom.

The singers capped it off like a holy choir, and the music swelled.

"K-Y-W… K-Y-W!"

And I cried. Hard. I just lost it. My heart was bursting with unembarrassed pride.

Alvy, still looking at Rhonda, jabbed me with his elbow. "Whoa, that babe is callin' my name. Tom-bo? Hey, wazzamatter? You okay, man?"

I sniffed, blinking. "Yeah... fine."

"Well, what's up then? You got a pain?"

I wiped my eyes with my coat sleeve. "No, no. But, Alvy, we gotta remember this. This exact second. Always. I mean... walkin' in here today, it's gonna completely change our lives, man."

Now, Alvis just wasn't built for epiphanies. He just bobbed his head, clueless, eyes darting, and shrugged. "Yeah... completely. So c'mon! Let's go!" He tugged the heavy glass door, and we stepped inside.

The place swallowed us. Leather couches gleamed like Cadillacs in the showroom, shiny fixtures winked in the light, and the air carried a peculiar perfume of cigarette smoke, floor polish, and ozone from who-knows-what electrical gadgetry was stuffed in the walls.

We'd never been in a broadcast station lobby before, and back then, we didn't know the half of it. This temple we worshiped was just a money machine. A business that pushed zit cream and sang "You're in the Pepsi Generation" commercials to our short attention spans. But to us? It was pure magic.

I dragged my hand along the couch, expecting to feel sparks fly. Alvy, less impressed, was already wagging his eyebrows at Rhonda like some bargain-bin Casanova. "Mama-mia!" he half-whispered as he ogled her tight blouse, "I wish I'd'a brought my X-ray specs."
I didn't laugh. Couldn't. My eyes locked on a glowing studio window off to the side, the sanctum behind soundproof glass where it all happened, where radio became something more than itself. "Hey! Look, man! Far out," I whispered.

At the mic sat a man with an undone skinny tie and rolled-up sleeves. He looked like a guy who could have worked for IBM. But he sure didn't.

"Oh, man! It's Jerry G.!" I yanked Alvy by his shirt collar.

We twisted a wall knob, and Jerry's voice bloomed from a speaker into the lobby.

"…Available at John Wade's in Shaker Square," Jerry said.

He spun a finger to his board-op, Phil, in a Hawaiian shirt, who pressed a cart button. The sound effect of a telephone ringing, followed by a pickup.

Jerry said, "Let me get that; it might be the phone. Yellow?"

Jerry flipped a switch, and instantly, his voice turned gravelly, as if he was on the other end of the phone.

"Hey, Jer! Sparky Sarnoff down at the transmitter," said Jerry's split personality.

A click switch, and back to the smooth, on-mic Jerry: "Yeah, Sparks, what now?"

"Yeah. I'm havin' seafood tonight with the wife."

A click, "Seafood, huh?" said Jerry.

And so it went, Jerry volleying with himself like a two-man comedy act. Until Sparky landed the punchline:

"So, Jer… You know how to steam clams?

Click. "No… how?"

"Make fun of their religion!"

A maniacal laugh from "Sparky," a sharp KYW jingle sting, and an angry hang-up sound effect, as Jerry shook his head like he was disappointed in mankind. "There's no doubt about it," he ad libbed, "I gotta start screenin' my calls!"

Phil finger-released a 45, and The Honeycombs filled the space. Jerry leaned in, buttery-smooth: "Jerry G. at three-fifty! And The Honeycombs demand to speak with their lawyer!"

And Jerry hit the vocal post on the nose. Up came the song with the perfectly set-up response of its opening lyric: "Have I right to hold you…"

Alvy clutched my sleeve. "NO! LOOK! That's wrong, see? The clock—it's 3:43! But he said three-fifty-three! That ain't right, Tommy."

I grinned, entranced. "Yeah. The man is righteously surreal."

"Maybe. 'Cept it still ain't right."

I thought Alvy was being a bit too judgmental. Maybe Jerry just made a boo-boo. I mean, it happens, right?

At the reception desk, Rhonda's voice snapped us back. "So! Can I help youse gentlemen?"

I stammered. "Yes, ma'am. We're, um, supposed to see Mister Keagels."

"Who?" She took the card, squinting. "Oh, youse mean Merk. Sure. Hold on."

She bent over the in/out sheet, and gravity took charge. Alvy's jaw hit the floor as he stared at Rhonda's large, and quite outstanding, breasts.

"So, this is… um, KYW A-M and F-M, huh?" he stammered. "And I bet'cha we're lookin' at two of the biggest… stations in town, right here."

"Yeah, they just might be," she said without looking up, lips curling around her cigarette.

"Oh, I do think so," Alvy whispered, eyes glued south of her neckline.

I jabbed him in the ribs and quickly shook my head without saying "Don't!"

She straightened and looked up, thankfully not catching where Alvy's eyes had landed. "Yeah. Merk's in a meetin'."

That "meetin'" was all smoke and shouting in a conference room just down the hall. Eleven salesmen in

94

mostly rumpled suits ringed a large oak table littered with graphs. A sign screamed: "Ratings = War!"

Merk leaned forward. "No, no. Look, Art. All's I'm sayin' is, what about the kids, huh? If we run too many damn commercials, we'll lose 'em."

Art Bocello, KYW Radio's general manager, slammed his manicured hands down hard, his diamond cuff links flashing. He was their tanned, white-haired leader in light blue Sansabelt pants. "NO! In this room, listeners come second. Our job—our ONLY job—is to sell a positive environment for products. Nothing else."

Merk's jaw tensed. "So, always the bottom line with you, is it?"

"Hell yes! It's a war out there, pal! And if you're smart, you'd best dummy up!"

Silence fell.

Back in the lobby, Alvy was shifting uncomfortably on the couch; a throw pillow on his jeans that covered a tented, erect and unexpected teenage problem. C'mon, he was a kid, and Rhonda was a real looker.

"Just go ask her," Alvy pleaded.

"All right. Jeez."

I shuffled up. "Uh, ma'am? Could we please use your, um, bath, um, restroom?"

Rhonda raised an eyebrow, crushed out her smoke, and buzzed the lock. "End of the hall, on the right."

We hustled off, Alvy still carried the pillow at his front pants nonchalantly as Rhonda watched with a questioning squint. We made it to the hallway. And as the door slammed behind us, Avy said, "My gawd, she's a freakin' Playboy centerfold, Tommy. Her F-M booby is killin' me down there!"

"Shh. All right, well, go on then. It's right over there." Alvy dropped the pillow camouflage and bee-lined toward the toilets. "Oh, thank you, Moses!" He said, quietly calling back, "I got some serious dog-floggin to do!"

Hooboy. Anyway, I passed by the closed double doors of the conference room. Voices continued to thunder inside. I peeked through a crack and heard talk of high ratings and "eating the lunch" of all KYW competitors.

Art said, "Cuz if there's one thing I learned in dubya-dubya deuce it's this: Anyone not with me on this ride is expendable!"

Merk said, "Look, man! I'm tellin' ya, the music means a lot to the kids. You want 'em to tune out?"

Ken, the program director, chimed in. "Merk! Merk, if I may. We still give kids the… presence, the, the perception of more music."

"There! See? And perception's reality!" said Art. "Shit, I'd put goddamn pig shit on this station if it'd attract a fuckin' audience! And I MEAN it!"

Art continued, "Which means I want this team to suck up every goddamned dollar a teenager has to spend with our sponsors! Now get the hell out and do your jobs!" And he stormed away, nearly bowling over Alvy, who had just returned from his emergency wank.

Alvy and Art exchanged a patriotic salute and an annoyed eye roll. I'll let you guess who did what.

Merk sighed, eyes darting to his watch. "Mark my words. He's gonna kill the damn golden goose," he said to one still-sitting salesman.

"Hi, Mr. Keagels, sir!" My hand shot out. "Um, remember us? Tommy and Alvy, from the other day?"

Merk looked confused, then sparked. "Oh yeah, you and short stuff! Sure! So, ah, yuns came, huh? Great! Well, then I guess it's time for the nickel tour, yeah, boys?"

Alvy and I nodded most enthusiastically, of course. "Great!" I said. "Thanks a lot, Mr. Keagels!"

Merk stopped short and squinted. "All right. Listen up good. Rule number one: Yuns always call me Merk, get me? Don't make me tell youse that again. We good? Okay then. C'mon, fallah me."

Just then, a new jingle rattled in my mind.

"Just call him Merk, not Mister Keagels! And now he is your boss! He's Dicky's Guardian Angel! So you better not piss him off!"

The tour began as we twisted through a maze of doors and corridors. First stop: the production studio—a room that smelled of smoke and somebody's half-eaten lunch. Dan, the engineer, was hunched over a turntable, stroboscope disc spinning hypnotically.

Merk commanded, "Tell 'em wha'cher doin' here, Danny-boy."

"Yeah. I, ah, I'm makin' sure the records we play spin about forty-seven, forty-eight rpm instead of at forty-five," he explained.

Alvy frowned. "Why? I mean, ain't they good like they are?"

"Ken says it makes the music sound brighter," Dan shrugged. "I, myself, don't hear it."

Merk smirked. "'Cept it shaves a few seconds off each tune. Enough for another commercial at the top of the hour. Yeah. 'Round here, that..." Merk paused, shrugged, and dropped his head, reliving the argument he'd lost with Art. He tousled Alvy's hair, then sighed, "That's... showbiz, kids."

Alvy wilted. I just nodded, filing it away as gospel.

Next stop: the studio control room. Jerry G.'s voice purred through the deejay booth as he pitched a "live read" for acne lotion.

"Picture this: It's a few days before a big swingin' date, right? And you're really turned on... Then you look in the mirror and, uh-oh, you're really turned off..."

Alvy wrinkled his nose. "That's unpossible. Why's Jerry sound like he's in Cleveland Stadium? He, he, he's like, in a closet, size'a my bathroom!"

"Maybe that's why the place always smells like cigarettes and wet crotch in there," Merk laughed.

Phil, the Hawaiian-shirted board op, chuckled and pointed at a rack of electronics. "It sounds so big cuz'a that: plate reverb. Makes a closet sound like Cleveland Stadium. Here, I'll show you."

Phil clicked a switch. Jerry's voice flattened, suddenly sounding dull and boxy. Then, with another flick, it bloomed back again—big, lush, perfectly equalized, and super ear-catching.

The hair on my arms stood up. "Whoa. That's neeto, huh?"

Alvy grimaced with disgust and whispered to me, "I guess. But it's still jus'… foolin' people."

Jerry wrapped with a flourish: "That's P-R-O P-A P-H! At all Cleveland area Gray Drug Stores!"

The ON AIR light winked off. But inside me, it kept glowing.

The next day, before we got to the station for our first day on the job, Merk told me what happened earlier with Dicky.

Out in front of KYW, just before his show, Dicky's battered VW Beetle sputtered to the curb. As he stepped out, trumpet in hand, his eyes lifted to a massive KYW billboard across the street promoting all of the station's on-air talent. Back then, some stations called their deejays "The Good Guys," or "The Boss Jocks," but at KYW, they were the V.I.P.s. For a moment, in Dicky's mind, all the deejays painted on the sign came alive—lipsyncing and cavorting among a bevy of beehived teenage girls prancing to the beat, and together they all sang the KYW V.I.P. Jingle:

"Yeah, yeah, yeah! We're the V.I.P.s. Yeah, yeah, yeah! Here to please…" they sang.

"Jerry G., boppin' at record hops; Jay Lawrence, spinnin' the latest pops; Martin and Howard, with comedy bits; "Swingin' Dicky Peppers, the fun never quits! On K-Y-W in Cleveland, Ohio! We're the V-I-Ps! Yeah, yeah, yeah!"

Then, without warning, Dicky's mind warped the scene. The Faceless Black Manikin appeared and swelled across the billboard, suffocating the air and swallowing color. Dicky stumbled back, panic on his face. He knew that Black Thing was after him again; it was one opponent he couldn't shake. He rushed toward the station entrance. When he dared to glance again, the horror had morphed back into just a billboard. Relieved, he peered through the lobby glass, saw Rhonda, and smiled.

Frankie Valli suddenly crooned, "Ronnie, Ronnie, you are my first love." In his new fantasy, Dicky glided toward her, spinning her and kissing her hand. They twirled and melted into an inseparable team, soft eyes for each other, and in perfect step. Then—there it was again, the Manikin, in the corner, leering, watching, waiting. A phonograph needle ripped across Dicky's mental soundtrack.

"DICK! HEY! Earth to DICKY!"

He found himself standing, confused, before Rhonda at reception. She waved a pink telephone note in front of his eyes and pointed a thumb over her shoulder.

"Here. Programming wants to see you. NOW."

In Ken's office, the reel-to-reel whirred, spilling out a sugary replay of the station's jingle singers: "K-Y-W, encore! Encore!" And then, brazen as a middle finger, The Kingsmen crashed in with "Louie, Louie," its thump tumbling into the room.

Over the intro came Dicky's unmistakable patter, slick and teasing: "Ten-twenty-two, at K-Y in Cleavage! Here's a 'Hit that Happened!' Our 'No-No of the Night!' Must be eighteen to listen! KINGSMEN...!"

The song barely had a chance to stretch its legs before Ken lunged for the controls and yanked the sound dead. Silence snapped down hard, broken only by the fizz of overhead lights. He stared across the desk at Dicky, fury radiating.

"That song is OFF our list, man, and you know it!" he barked.

Dicky raised his palms, eyes darting, the faintest grin tugging at his lips. "Okay, but, but I was makin' a point about… y'know, censorship."

Ken shot forward in his chair. "No, no, no, no. NO! I pick the songs, Dick, me! I decide when and what gets played, not you, not anyone else—me!"

"I, I know, but… " Dicky's protest came out weak, childlike.

Ken wasn't having it. "Playin' music from home? Really? You want to get hauled up in front of some committee like that Jew-bastard, Freed!? You know them lyrics are bein' investigated by the F-fuckin'-B-I! We could be fined, for Chrissakes!"

He scooped up a stack of pink callback slips and shook them in Dicky's face. "And look! Look'a this! I got sponsors, I got Westinghouse Corporate, I got lawyers, I got the goddamn Catholic Church sayin' you're corruptin' the youth of Cleveland!' Man, you gotta come off less radical, and more… I dunno, wacky, Dick. That's the character you play, that's the persona I hired. Fun, trendy. A lightning rod for all the stupid shit kids are into—clothes, music…"

Dicky smirked. "Sex?"

Ken paused in mid-screed. "Yeah, but not "Louie Louie" sex!" He snapped, then relented. "All right, maybe sometimes you work a little blue—I mean, ya gotta keep an edge, I get that—but use the double entendres as seasoning, man. A pinch goes a long way. Everything's focused here, Dicky, controlled. Everything on our air is done for a good goddamn reason."

Dicky deflated, mumbling, "Sure. Okay. I… I'm sorry, Ken."

A beat and a conman's stare shot from Ken's eyes.

"Sorry? I don't want you to be sorry! I want you to… keep up the good work!" Ken's voice softened, conspiratorial now. "By the way, I never said that. For all Art or anyone else knows, I gave you a good ass reamin' today. And I also swear I never said what I'm about to say: this response is phenomenal, man! You're radio's new bad boy, Dick! My, my, high school greaser dressed like a preppy! That's what I want! It's edgy, rebellious! It's fuckin' anarchy! And you know who loves stupid shit like this?"

"The... kids?"

Ken grinned, wolfish. "*The Cleveland Press*! The Plain Dealer! Screw WHK! Screw all the competition! You're our goddamn fifth Beatle, man! But—and I say this from the heart—just play the fuckin' songs on the list."

The words hung heavy, half-threat, half-praise, the fine line between Ken's rage and admiration drawn as thin as the magnetic tape that had carried "Louie Louie" into the room.

Back at home that night after the tour and just before dinner, Dad slapped the evening paper on the Formica table, his voice thick with suspicion. "Nah, nah. Look at what you jus' told me here. A man comes to town, changes his name, why? Cuz he's happy and proud? No. He's hidin' somethin'. That ain't good."

I tried to explain, maybe too quickly. "No, no. See, his real name is Richard Paprykarz Jr."

"Yeah, so what's wrong wit that? At'sa nice Polack name," Dad said.

"Okay, but the station changed it, see? He goes by Dicky Peppers on the air."

Dad cross-examined, "Exactly my pernt? Why? How's come?

"Well… because a good on-air name can, you know, make a deejay's career. Like 'Wolfman Jack.'"

Dad sputtered, "A wolf?"

"Ooo, cuz Jack's a big, scary animal, huh?" Mom said.

"Wait, wait, wait," said Dad. "So you're tellin' me this, this here Peppy guy, he's a dirty grifter, then."

"NO! All the big stars get new radio names," I said in frustration. "Aw, Dad, you don't understand showbiz."

Dad's face reddened, a storm rising. "Hey, I understand right and wrong! And tell me this: how's come these jagoffs ain't got normal names like, y'know, 'Fats' Licavoli, or Henry Stinkowitz? WHY? Cuz they

ALL gotta have Johnny Bull names to kiss up to the man! I say, where's the Union on this, huh? Adelaide, help me out here."

Mom, loyal but weary, chimed in from her chair. "Yeah, spinnin' up the songs faster, Tommy, that's just… naughty."

Carmel, kneeling on her chair, wriggled her rear end at me like she was about to broadcast in smell-o-vision.

"CarMEL?!" Mom snapped, horrified.

My sister grinned. "Tell 'em what else they do with the songs, dodo bird."

"Hey, he ain't extinct," Mom retorted.

"Yet," Dad grumbled.

Mom turned back to me, pressing. "Well? Come on. What?"

I shrugged, surrendering. "Okay… so, every hour the deejay's gotta play the number one song again."

Dad's eyes bulged. "What? The same song? Over and over?"

"That can't be right," Mom muttered.

"S' craziness!" Dad thundered.

"And they sell the air to people!" Carmel blurted, piling it on, nearly hysterical. "They sell people bags of air!"

"AIR!" Dad exploded, throwing up his hands. "Christ! It, it's like that ol' Brooklyn Bridge scam!"

I snapped at Carmel, my cheeks hot. "No! I told you, it's for the commercials, numb-nuts!"

"EH!" Dad roared. "You do NOT mention boy's... t, t, tentacles in front'a your mother!"

He leaned in close, his voice dropping to a dangerous growl. "All right, you listen to me, kid. I may not know the showbidnes, but I know bunco when I smell it. This here's the long con, boy! That's what 'em cheats is pullin'. They're gettin' inside your head, see? They ain't playin' records, they're playin' you! Like a tree-card monte on the street. And, and, you—you're the mark, Tommy! The patsy! It's, it's a, a flam-flim! A big lie! And I forbid you from ever goin' to that goddamn rotten place again!"

He shoved back his chair, the legs screeching on linoleum, and stood with finality. His eyes swept across us, sharp and condemning, and a little bit confused. "Ahhch! All youse kids is nothin' but suckers!"

Then he stormed out, disgust trailing behind him.

For a moment, the kitchen hung in silence. My eyes stung, and the tears squeezed free no matter how hard I fought them. Mom reached over and laid her hand on mine, her voice a whisper of comfort. "I'll… talk to your father."

FOUR — "On the Air, EVERYWHERE!"

"If you want to find the secrets of the universe, think in terms of frequency and vibration." — Nikola Tesla

The bus brakes squealed like banshees, and we tumbled out near the KYW studios, ready for our first big night of helping produce Dicky's show, ON AIR, live!

Later, Mom would be waiting in our Rambler, headlights off, ready to scoop us up before Dad ever got home. Fortunately, back then, my Dad worked a semi-permanent three to eleven shift at Republic Steel in the Flats—and often pulled doubles, too. Which meant me and Alvy could take a bus to the radio station after dinner, then catch a ride back with Mom, and Dad would NEVER know! Yep. It was the perfect crime.

A horn blared. Some Studebaker with a souped-up V-8 screeched by us. Alvis froze in the street, mitten up like a traffic cop.

"Why, ya no good prick!" He yelled.

I staggered to the curb. "Sorry!" I hollered at the driver, who shot off in a cloud of exhaust.

Only then did Alvis peel back the mitten to reveal his secret: one pale middle finger saluted the departing car. We doubled over, gasping with laughter, and raced for KYW's front doors. Yeah, Alvy was a cool groover. He had a lot more courage than me, and I love him for it.

Merk was already stationed at the Ansaphone booth, a glorified closet wedged right next to Dicky's on-air studio. In there, automatic answering machines took listener requests.

Merk showed us how things work. On the wall, a dog-eared Cleveland White Pages leaned against a pushpin map, suburbs speared with thumbtacks. Three stumpy black telephones squatted on the counter, each one wired into what KYW called "state-of-the-art" 1960s technology. To us, it looked like something cooked up by NASA.

The Ansaphone machines themselves were gray metal boxes with blinking lights, recording on small reel-to-reel tapes. Every time a call came in, a pair of thin metallic arms would jerk to life, sliding neatly under the phone's receiver. The machine would lift the handset—so polite, like a butler answering the door—then record a caller's message, and drop the receiver back into place. Next call. Next voice.

Our job was simple enough: write down first names and high schools, and feed them to Dicky. This way, he could shout them out on air and make every teenager from Sandusky to Strongsville believe they were part of "Pepper's People." For me, it was fun. A little factory line of magic. But Alvy? He couldn't take the pressure.

I caught him twisting a string of broken recording tape around its reel, nervously winding it like a string of rosary beads. His eyes darted toward the glass window looking straight into the deejay booth.

"This is a catastrophe, man," he moaned. "Jeez! I'm goin' mental with this."

Through the glass, you could see Dicky Peppers in his kingdom; his show had just started. Chick, his studio control room board operator, a very sweet man with a bad toupee, pointed to a wall clock to remind Dicky to do a time check.

The clock read 7:13 p.m., plain as day. And there was Dicky, leaning into the mic, his voice as young and exciting as ever. The Sonovox chimed with a sing-song: Hubba-hubba!

"It's seven twenty-three, hubba-hubba time, with your Swingin' Dicky on K-Y!" The "sexy woman" drop-in underscored the line with a coital, "Oooh! Mmmm." Alvy glanced at the clock and winced.

Music swelled—a Manfred Mann cut, "Doo-Wah-Diddy." Dicky laughed into the mic. The music rose, drowning everything else.

Alvy slapped his forehead. "Shit. Again? Tommy! He does it again!"

"What?"

That's when Merk barged in, another typed list clutched in his fist. "C'mon, yuns two, hurry it up!"

Alvy pounced, desperate for answers. "Hey, Merk. How's come Dicky always tells the time wrong?"

Merk didn't miss a beat. "Aw, top management bullshit, kid. Somethin' about ratings."

"Ratings?"

"Yeah, if Dicky picks up, like, five minutes in every quarter hour, the station wins. It's some… advertising thing. Now, let's go."

"But… but then he, he's lyin' to people," Alvis said.

Merk wheeled on him. "What are you, Shorty, Mister Clock? Nobody got the right time no more? Look, I got, ah, quarter after. You?"

I checked my Timex. "Seven thirty-two. But I like to be early."

Merk pointed at Alvy with his cigarette. "You?"

Alvy raised a bare wrist. "The Speidels give me a rash."

"See? Who cares? It's time, and time's passin', so c'mon!"

I frowned. "Um, Merk, what if we can't understand names on the tape? Some are… garbled."

"Make 'em up."

Alvis blinked and pulled a face. "What?"

"Yeah. Or copy a bunch from these here white pages." Merk jabbed at the fat directory with his thumb.

"It's why they're there. Ken wants it to sound like everybody's tuned in. So Dicky needs lots'a names, and lots'a high schools. Which reminds me…" He shoved the list closer. "Here's a batch'a school names. Rotate 'em."

"And how 'bout song requests?" I asked.

"No requests."

Alvis looked stricken. "NO! But, I mean, we always tell people to call with dedications…"

"Razzle-dazzle, my boy," Merk barked. "Now hurry it up! Dicky needs names and schools, chop-chop!"

Alvy pursed his mouth, side-eyed me, and shook his head.

But so it went. The phones clanged, the tape spun, and our pencils scratched names onto slips, real and imagined. That was our assembly line, and Merk was our foreman. Out there, Dicky Peppers made it sound like a city of teenagers adored him. In here, it was two kids in a smoke-stained closet, learning how radio really got made. And God help me, I felt as though I'd landed in heaven.

Dicky's first hour waned; we did our thing, and the clock approached eight o'clock.

Down the corridor, through the glass of the news booth, Jon Scott Trotter, a nebbishy, balding fella with coke-bottle glasses, who looked to be sixty but had to be in his late thirties, was about to "present" what was considered news on a Top 40 station back then. The man was born to narrate. He could have announced a kindergarten ballet recital and made it sound momentous.

Trotter settled himself in front of the mic, put on his headphone cans, and began the ritual: tapping the foot pedal, testing something called a MacKenzie Endless Repeater that spat out sharp one-second blasts—dit-dit-dit-dit-dit-dit-dit-dit—that would separate news stories. He gave Chick the thumbs-up as if they were about to launch the Mercury capsule into space.

Chick, hunched in the control room, dropped a long, heavy tonearm onto a giant sixteen-inch turntable with a dedicated transcription platter on it. The thing was so wide it looked like it could serve a family of six. On the label, the giant disc read: Teletype/Newsroom SFX.

Chick flipped the talk-back switch, and his voice filtered through the intercom.

"In ten, Jonny…"

Trotter cleared his throat with the sort of dramatic flair only a man in love with his own pipes could summon—loud coughs, guttural blats, snorts, gravelly "blah-wha-wahs." Like a bullfrog gargling gravel.

"Doo-Wah-Diddy" ended cold. Chick hit the first of two big, attention-getting news sounders, rolled the teletype under it, and pointed the cue. Showtime!

Trotter leaned into the mic with the gravitas of Walter Cronkite on crack: "A-tisket-a-tasket, a BABY found DEAD in a BASKET!"

He chopped the air, then jabbed a finger at Chick for the next thunderclap sounder.

"THAT story tops K-Y-W News BANNER LINES!"

Back went Trotter's foot to the pedal—dit-dit-dit-dit-dit-dit-dit. And then he really took off!

"CLEVELAND!" he roared. "The city's finest called to an icy east-side flop house tonight. Our Boys in

Blue burst in—guns drawn, ready to spit fire—and find a frozen kid-sicle! Coroner rules hypothermia. C-Town detectives yell, HOMICIDE! The strung-out polar parents charged with murder in the minus one degree. Cold Case Closed!"

Another stomp of the pedal. Dit-dit-dit-dit-dit-dit-dit.

"AKRON!" he bellowed. "A single-engine plane nosedives into a hovel at University Heights! CRASH! SPLAT! In-FERRR-nooooh! Smoke-eaters are on the scene!"

That was Trotter's and KYW's "news style," never to be confused with The New York Times. Always a bit too eager to sell the sizzle, even if the steak was a tragedy. I guess Ken thought if K-Y had to stop the music, they'd better at least make it, um, "interesting" for the kids.

Meanwhile, in the deejay booth, Dicky sat oblivious to the carnage across the glass. He was hunched over his tiny console, nose buried in Camus' *The Fall*—a story about tortured souls in the last circle of hell and the nature of nonexistence. I know, right?

Merk nudged him with all the subtlety of a cattle prod, sliding a bright red pill under his nose and dangling a cup of joe in the other hand. I watched it all from the Ansaphone booth, wondering what gives?

"Here," Merk said. "It's time."

Dicky didn't even flinch. "Hey, I'm readin' here."

"No, no, c'mon. Y'know the drill."

"Actually, I feel pretty good right now, man."

"Uh-uh. You'll be draggin' by the fourth hour if you don't. And I'm watchin' this time. So, c'mon!"

Dicky surrendered, popped the pill, and chased it with a slurp. He made a face, Camus slipping from his focus. "Happy now?"

"Open," Merk ordered.

"Merk, really—"

"Open!"

Back in the news booth, Trotter was still hammering the pedal—dit-dit-dit-dit-dit—and thundered, "Weather in a word: Clouds! K-Y-Sky-Watch just ahead of 'Much More MUUUUUUUUuuuuu-sic'…" The man gasped for breath, nearly choking on his own baritone. "...in a moment!"

He flung the cue toward Chick, who slid in a commercial.

Dicky, meanwhile, opened his mouth reluctantly, caught between duty and indignation. Merk peered in like a dentist, checking for noncompliance.

"Tongue."

In the control room, Chick's filtered voice cut through the speaker: "Comin' back in sixty, boys."

Dicky's mouth snapped shut, glared at Merk. "Jesus, you're an asshole, you know that?"

"I do." Merk smiled, smug as a cat. "TONGUE!" Dicky stuck it out, resentful as a kid at the pediatrician's office.

And then, just for punctuation, Merk banged on the glass, hollering into the Ansaphone booth where Alvis and I sat scribbling down caller names like dutiful clerks of the kingdom. "HEY, YUNS TWO! NOW! LET'S GO!"

And that, folks, was KYW: dead babies in baskets, Camus in the control room, pep pills down the hatch, and Trotter turning the weather into a Wagnerian opera. Looking back, I'm not sure whether to laugh or weep. But it sure beat working in a steel mill.

"C'mon! C'MON!" Merk barked, half-muffled by the glass, half in his desperate, exasperated tone. We grabbed all the names and notes we took, blasted around the corner, and down the hall.

Alvy tried to hustle, but hustling was not his physical gift. His sneakers squeaked on the linoleum, his stubby legs folding like bowling pins. Then, with a grace that was purely accidental, he flailed, and the neat stack of song requests went airborne. Pages fluttered like ticker tape celebrating Alvy's failure.

Merk opened Dicky's studio door and clutched his head. "Jeez, youse two! COME ON!"

We scrambled, all knees and elbows, scooping paper off the floor. Alvis stuffed a crumpled one under his armpit and finally—breathing like he'd just finished a marathon—lurched toward Merk, who snatched the stack without making eye contact and shot through the doorway to Dicky's booth.

"That's Action Central K-Y-Double News!" Trotter boomed. His words hit with polished tones—an alarm wrapped in caramel.

Meanwhile, in studio control, Chick leaned forward over the giant console, a reflection of VU meters bouncing green and gold across his glasses. He flicked a switch, and his voice filtered into Dicky's headphones:

"Standby, Pep!"

Everything in that building vibrated like a rocket revving for takeoff.

Back in the news booth, Trotter ramped up the outro. "Next report at any moment! When news breaks out, we break in!"

In the deejay booth, Dicky grabbed a sheaf of requests in one hand and, with the other, lifted the trumpet.

"I'm Jon Scott Trotter," the newscaster chimed, never missing a beat, "standing by for the World's Greatest Trumpet Player on... the Swingin' Dicky Peppers Show!"

That was the cue. Chick hit the jingle donut, a perfect ring of brass and a jingle chorus. His finger snapped on Dicky's mic live and pointed. The ON AIR sign above the booth door lit up like Judgment Day, red and unforgiving.

Dicky lifted the horn and let it rip—

HONK!

The jingle singers swooped in.

"You're hearing things!"

A Sonovox voice dropped in, sounding like a singing steel guitar, teasing:

"You're hearing things!"

The singers doubled down, rolling into the call letters like it was scripture:

"With K-Y-W's Swingin' Dicky Peppers! Swing Dicky, Swing!"

Exciting, upbeat music swelled under their voices, the kind of brassy bed that made your heart accelerate.

"Hubba-hubba," Dicky boomed, grinning as though every listener was his co-conspirator. "From your Guru of Horn-some-ness! A big K-Y welcome to Joleen and Gunner in Sandusky tonight!"

My memory camera pushes in close on Dicky, closer still, until all I can see is the glisten of his lips at the mic. Then—like Alice tumbling down the rabbit hole—I'm inside the wire mesh itself, swallowed by the microphone and carried along with the voice.

"Kathy, Jacky, Joe, Betsy, and the great Senior Class at Rocky River—Go Pirates!" His voice ricocheted everywhere at once. "Hi and hubba-hubba to Mary Grace at Beaumont High—Whooo!"

In my mind, live action morphed to a cartoon: electrified atoms sparked across circuits and lit up an invisible highway of technology.

"Hiyo, and 'Turn Into Peanut Butter' from Kelly and Ginny in Strongsville, and 'Big Bad John' listenin' all the way down in Pittsboro, North Carolina, tonight! STUNNER!"

The signal streaked past switches, buzzed through sound limiters, and squeezed against audio compressors.

"Comin' to you ALIVE from the great Midwestern Port City of Cleveland!" Dicky crowed. "With me, your Swingin' Dicky!

I could see the current now, molten light shooting into a water-cooled transmitter, its tubes as big as gallon milk jugs. Warning signs flashed: DANGER! 50,000 WATTS!

"Hubba-hubba!" Screamed the Sononox.

The charge pulsed into ground cables, then climbed the broadcast tower, higher and higher, red airplane beacons flashing, a metronome against the night.

"So buckle up your security blankets," he announced, "'cause Pepper's People are on the air EVERYWHERE!"

The jingle singers returned, triumphant.

"From Canada to Florida, Ohio, and the U.S.A. loves Swingin' Dicky Peppers on K-Y-W in Cleveland, Ohio!"

The Sonovox chuckled one more time.

"Whooop-peee!"

And right on its tail, the music kicked in—the Beatles, "Can't Buy Me Love." The record spun hot, filling every corner of the Midwest... and, to me, the known world.

Golden waves pulsed from the tower, flooding across the sprawl of Cleveland, arcing past suburbs and highways, flying over the Cuyahoga River's steel mills.

Out in Parma, front porch lights glowed on identical rows of boxy ranch houses, each one tuned to the same piece of invisible sky. And over all of it, like a shared hallucination, came the Beatles' backbeat, cutting through walls and windows.

On the west side, in Rocky River, a pack of high school seniors crammed into somebody's parents' rec room. Somebody's mom had baked a sheet cake, and somebody's dad had opened a Schlitz. But the real guest of honor was Dicky's voice, pouring from an old Sony TR-63. He'd called them out by name—Kathy, Jacky, Joe, Betsy—and suddenly, immortality was theirs. For one moment, Rocky River was the center of the universe. They whooped so loud the neighbors called to complain.

Down in Strongsville, Kelly and Ginny perched on the hood of a '58 Chevy parked by the Dairy Queen, a transistor balanced between them. When Dicky read out their request—"Turn into Peanut Butter"—they squealed like someone had just proposed marriage. Passersby laughed, but the girls didn't care. They'd been heard on the radio.

And way down in Pittsboro, North Carolina—because the signal traveled that far on a clear night—Big Bad John sat on a porch swing, chain-smoking Pall Malls and tapping his boot. "Stunner," Dicky had called it, and damn if that didn't put a smile on a man who hadn't smiled in weeks.

Electric voices in the night, flying through thin air. A wall of sound leaping into the dark and finding you, no matter where you were. Radio was miraculous, man! A full-on, raise-the-dead miracle! The hype, the thrill of knowing this invisible force was slipping into bedrooms, basements, and parked cars all at once, lit a fire inside me.

Everywhere you listened, there was Dicky, the omnipresent, horn-happy deity of the airwaves. He was Cleveland's Pied Piper, and we were all rats in letter jackets, beehive hairdos, and go-go boots, frugging to his tune.

Like a Roman candle, that signal just kept going—past Parma and Shaker Heights, past Lakewood's crowded taverns, past the darkened sprawl of the Collinwood rail yards, and out across Lake Erie, where Canadian freighters cut through dark waters.

The signal bounced east, brushing the rolling hills of Pennsylvania. They shot west, kissing Toledo goodnight. They leapt across state lines, where kids in Buffalo huddled under blankets and whispered "Hubba-hubba" in an improbable Cleveland accent.

I swear, you could chart the geography of adolescence by where those signals landed. That's what radio did: it shrank the world and blew it wide open, all at once.

Sure, radio also told a lot of little white lies. It hyped products no kid could afford, promised glamour most would never achieve, and painted the drab world a shade shinier than it really was. But the lies were wrapped around a bigger truth: connection. Somebody out there was listening, same as you. And that—believe me—could save a kid's life.

And in the booth, Dicky was in his kingdom, feeding us one outrageous line after another, backed by the safest of "dangerous music." I grant you, it was all smoke and mirrors. But the effect? Oh man, the effect on me was as true as it gets.

Why? Because, and here's the dirty little secret: I wanted this time, my time, to be special. Not just to watch from the hallway, clutching somebody else's song requests. I wanted in. To be part of the magic. To bend the airwaves with my voice, my own touch of madness. To make some poor kid under a blanket tap out a song's beat on his little dog's belly.

Back inside the KYW control room, Chick kept the platters spinning. His hands moved like a magician's, knobs fading, carts popping, levels riding the sweet spot between overload and perfection. Merk darted in and out of hallways like a courier in a war zone, grabbing more requests, ready to shove them under Dicky's nose like telegrams from the president.

And Dicky? He held court. Honking his trumpet and cracking jokes that didn't so much make sense as make sound. That was his spectacular gift. And me—Tommy Bianco, a few months shy of thirteen—was stuck just outside the circle, watching. This was no ordinary job. It wasn't steel mills or podiatry. It was alchemy.

Later that night, it was time for Dicky's most hilarious and interactive bit. A daily check-in with his listeners called "Rate a Joke."

"It's your Swingin' Dicky Peppers Show!" He declared, his trumpet blasting. "Where it's time to communicate together telephonically! Let's go to the laugh lines and…"

Dicky pushed a button on a flashing phone bank.

"…Rate a Joke!" he commanded.

The line clicked. A voice, flat and raw, spat, "Aw, bite me!"

Dicky froze, one eyebrow cocked, then licked his lips with dangerous calm. "Sure. Gimme your address?"

The Sonovox machine—Chick's toy—dropped a greasy burp of sound: "Hubba-hubba!"

Chick burst out laughing. Dicky killed the line with a sharp hang-up and rolled straight to the next.

"What a TEASE! Rate a Joke!"

This time, a reedy voice smirked, "So there was this boy ghost and this really sexy girl ghost, right?"

"Mah-huh?" Dicky's laughing eyes, in a snap, turned wary. They flicked toward studio control and stared blankly in terror. I saw the moment, but what was happening? I imagined that there—impossible, silent, and perched like a nightmare—stood the Faceless Black Manikin again. Right behind Chick. Watching. Its blank head tilted. What the eff, man?

I saw Dicky's grin collapse, as if gravity itself had betrayed him. Dicky shut his lids tight and swallowed hard.

The caller droned on: "And the boy ghost says, 'Hey babe, as a female ghost, do you like to tap on walls?'"

Dicky's face clenched, flush with sweat. Shaking his head slowly, as if he didn't want to look, but his eyes fluttered open. The Thing was gone. Chick scratched his nose, oblivious, the room perfectly normal.

"Girl ghost goes, 'Sure!'" the caller chuckled.

Dicky silently exhaled and sank back into his chair.

"And the boy ghost says, 'Well, why don't you come over to my house and we can bang on the floor!'"

A cue pointed; Chick's hand obediently slapped a button.

"Two, two, two, two..." bleated the Sonovox's joke rating number.

"Hubba-hubba!" Dicky barked, voice an octave higher than he'd like.

The jingle singers rescued him: "If it's goin' on—it's goin' on K-Y-W in Cleveland, Ohio!"

Chick slip-cued a spinning 45, as brass and drums exploded into "Dancing in the Street."

Dicky recovered his mask of bravado and roared over the intro: "Here I thought seven to eleven was my time slot—turns out it's the I.Q. of my listeners! Martha Reeves! Spincerely yours!"

And the music enveloped him, giving him time to clamp a hand to his forehead and rub off the fear.

Yeah, I saw it all, and it clearly registered, but I shrugged it off, assigning it no profound meaning at the time. Maybe it was nothing, a hiccup of a previous thought Dicky had, like, "Shit, I haven't paid my rent." I mean, I was only a kid. But it puzzled me, and after years of turning that moment over and over in my mind, I sensed Dicky had seen something that night that no one else had. Something beyond frightening was conjured from the recesses of his mind. To this day, I can only imagine the burden of carrying such unremitting horror.

But when Dicky said "Pepper's People are on the air everywhere!" I believed him. Not just in him, but in the "everywhere." The promise that I, too, might one day be more than a kid with static in his ears.

That's what radio was for me: not just sound, but a solemn promise. And that night, with Top 40 hits rattling the glass and jingles still echoing in my head, I knew—I just knew—I'd spend the rest of my life chasing that signal.

That was the dream. That was the drug. And there was no going back.

Five — Alvy's Conscience

"Man is least himself when he talks in his own person.
Give him a mask… —Oscar Wilde

om waited where she always did, parked crooked just outside the KYW building. The station's call letters coughed a tired halo over a city that worked in shifts and never quite slept.

She drove our old two-tone Rambler—white and a sort of powder blue that had given up trying to be either the powder or the blue. It was hard to tell. The heater was running on low, and Mom was knitting—click-click, click-click—yarn skeining out from a bag like a magician's endless scarf. I swear she could knit in her sleep, needles tapping time to KYW's Top 10 countdown leaking through the car's slightly open driver's-side window.

Alvy and I shot out of the building, sprinted to the car, shoes slapping damp concrete. It felt both illicit and blessed at once. Remember now: we'd bus to the station, then have my Mom pick us up later, way before

Dad ever got home. The perfect setup. (I don't recommend perfect setups; they're just rehearsals for consequences.)

Inside the Rambler, cracks split through worn vinyl seats. Mom waved and beckoned to us. Alvy and I jumped in and got comfortable. In the back, Carmel had surrendered to sleep, her head making a pillow of Walter's rear end.

"So, whad'ja you two learn today, hm?" Mom asked.

"Maaahm!" Carmel groaned, eyes closed. "I'm SLEEEPIN' over here!"

"All right, sassy-ass!" Mom snapped back, her knitting never missing a purl.

"But, Maaahm…"

"SHH! So help me God, Carmel-Jean, I will set you outside and smack you with this car door."

She let that hang, then turned her attention toward me and Alvy, eyebrows raised. "Okay, so tell me everything!"

Alvy was quiet, head down. I was primed to testify. "Well, tonight we actually used the deejay's bathroom!"

Her hand went to her chest. "No!"

"Oh yeah," I said, already riding the lift of the memory. "We really did!" It was etched in my mind like scrimshaw.

The deejay's men's room had two urinals, a stall with a door that didn't quite latch, and tile grout the color of old teeth. It smelled of urinal cakes and disinfectant, both losing the battle. Oh, and somebody had taped a pin-up calendar inside one of the stalls—March, the month of false promises. Fluorescent lights zizzed and flickered, adding a bit of a horror movie vibe.

I took my place before a chipped porcelain trough as if I was riding a pony and let 'er fly. The stream's echo climbed the walls but came back to me like applause. In those seconds, I swore I was plugged into some royal lineage.

"Wow!" I said, gently swaying as if some invisible Cleveland Indians game organist had hit a chord just for me. "This, this is like a, a, miracle, Alv. It really is, huh?"

"Yeah, sure." Alvy scowled. He was having a day. He'd unzipped, reached in—then stalled at the intersection of Fabric and Fastener.

"I mean, look'a me!" I said, giddy with triumph. "I'm peein'! No hands! Right where all the great men of radio have also stood and peed before me!"

"Damn!" He said, grimacing at the zipper. "I hate husky pants. I told my Ma, my fingers is too nubby to grab my wiener in husky pants. The woman buys me husky pants."

That's friendship for you: one kid sees a miracle, the other loses a wrestling match to his trouser snake.

So, that was my heavily cool KYW bathroom story. And off we drove, dropping Alvy off at his house and chugging home.

Here I must switch gears. Now, we're in Dicky's apartment. Since we're here—since the story wants to go where it goes—you might fairly ask how I knew what happened the rest of that night. Well, I didn't. Not really. Remember, I was twelve, but very close to being a real teenager (as I'd let everyone at school know). No, I wasn't in Dicky's apartment, but I knew what happened in there because, well, a radio station "leaks" and not just in the men's room. I mean by gossip that shakes walls. By the truth people reveal when they think they're just jokin' around. By the two pill bottles Merk guarded like a talisman, and by the way Dicky's eyes sometimes darted toward spaces that had nothing in them.

Mostly, I got my scuttlebutt out in the parking lot from Chick, Dicky's board-op. He told me behind-the-scenes stories the public didn't need to know. Like Chick, I learned to hear what's beneath the music. So, here was the hot goss:

You remember Rhonda, the station receptionist with the massive jugs? Well, let's say Dicky and she enjoyed each other's company A LOT! Besides, Dicky left a trail of evidence like breadcrumbs. Over the years, I scotch-taped together fragments of the rumors I'd heard to make sense. Not a courtroom record, but a form of truth the way radio creates it: performed into being.

So—picture this with me.

Dicky's apartment rode high over Lake Erie, eighteenth floor, where the wind blows in the faint smell of fish, and waves relentlessly chew the shore in the dark. Dicky never had much furniture. He was a deejay, a vagabond, and lived a nomadic life. What mattered was a few pairs of shoes, shirts, pants, a couple of ties, and, of course, all his books. Pretty much everything he could stuff inside a VW Bug when he left for a better-paying gig. Most working deejays, by the way, only hang around eighteen months or so at any station, which means they need to travel light. Yep, the only way to move up in radio is to move on.

Inside, a pizza box sat open on the coffee table, with beer bottles like exclamation points at the edge of a rented couch. An open fifth of bourbon sat on the floor, and a mound of half-smoked ciggys overflowed the ashtray. And—neat as two white train tracks—lines of unsnorted cocaine, which back then, was radio's newest drug of choice. All that and a bag of primo marijuana.

In the bedroom, Dicky lay atop an unseen woman—a shape under a sheet. You guessed it. It was Rhonda, frustrated and very human. Dicky sweats, pumps, grunts. He's almost there; then he stops between floors. Nothing. He quivers, shudders, a body forgetting how to end a sentence.

"Ahhch! Goddamnit!

He pulls out and does a graceless spin-flop onto the mattress beside her, his robe in a sad heap at the foot of the bed, his pride somewhere under it.

"Sorry," he says, not looking at her.

Rhonda shrugs the way people do when they don't want to make a problem bigger. She reaches to the nightstand, shakes a cigarette free, and lights up. The first inhale settles her face into something like acceptance.

"Dicky, if ain't I doin' somethin' you like, I…"

He waves the smoke away. "No, no. It, it's not you, Ronnie. It's… these goddamn pil—"

POUNDING! Loud pounding! A fist with an attitude hammers the front door.

Rhonda yanks the sheet to her breasts. Dicky grabs his robe, laces it as he goes, his man parts waning but still alive enough to be embarrassed.

As he's about to turn the corner from the bedroom, something in the window catches him. The Faceless Black Manikin looks in from the night—from the eighteenth floor!—and somehow it hovers there, patient, relentless, and impossible. No face, just the idea of a head. Dicky sees it. Concern rides his bones; a thick fear sucks all the air from the room. He freezes, hearing his racing heartbeat. He blinks, and perspiration forms on his forehead and above his lips. He swallows hard and looks again. The pane is back to glass, and the lake below is just cold water without a human soul.

Dicky opens the front door unkindly. "WHAT!?"

It's Merk. Of course, it's Merk. He eyes the robe with a quick glance. "Oh, I see you're still up," Merk says, deadpan, like the punchline built into Dicky's name: Yeah, that's "Swingin' Dicky" all right!

Dicky's hands fumble with the robe tie, covering a body that insists on humiliating him at every opportunity. "Shit, Merk! C'mon! Christ, it's one-thirty!"

"Ehh, I was in the neighborhood."

Rhonda appears at the bedroom doorway, wrapped in the sheet. Merk gives her a small finger wave: hello, goodbye, and don't get comfortable.

He leans toward Dicky, voice turned down. "Man. How many times I gotta say it: You don't shit where you eat."

Rhonda hears the slur and answers it with a door slam that resents every vowel.

Merk steps into the living room without asking—he's "the handler," not a guest—eyes scanning. Open pizza box. Beer bottles. Bourbon. Powder on glass cut with an American Express card.

"Really?"

"What? It's… dinner."

"Hm, and dessert," Merk says, pointing to the nose candy.

"Yeah. S'from Juggy, y'know, the record guy at Wand."

"Sure. I know the fuckin' turd."

"C'mon, it's jus' a little thank you for the 'Louie, Louie' thing."

Merk's jaw tightens. He can already see the headlines. "This is goddamn dangerous shit, man! You still don't get it, do you? You're on the bubble here, Dick. Both our jobs is on the line if you don't do what you're fuckin' told! Hold on."

From his jacket, Merk pulls out a pill bottle. The plastic clicks as he shakes a blue one into his palm. Dicky glances at the living room drapes. There It is again—the Faceless Black Manikin, a dark oval head and the hint of a tilt, a curiosity without eyes. Panic rises on the back of Dicky's neck. He looks away—as if you can ever win by not looking—and when he looks back, it's vanished.

"Here," Merk says. "Eat this. It'll help you sleep."

"How 'bout I jus' spark up some grass?"

"Take… the pill."

Dicky, miserably obedient, pops the blue pill and chases it with a swig of bourbon.

From the bedroom, the sheet whispers; Rhonda has the door cracked, watching the scene. Merk began his inspection.

"Open. Tongue. Cheeks. C'mon."

Dicky relents. He's learned that there are worse humiliations than being alive.

So, that was the story, as I understood it, at least. Was it true? After hearing—and seeing—all the other things that happened, I think it was. And I promise I'll get to those other things later.

The next night after dinner, I waited for Alvy at the bus stop, bouncing on my heels, jacket collar turned up against the wind. The city at dusk smelled of cooked cabbage and bus fumes. Back at KYW, Roy Orbison was singing "It's Over" on my transistor. Like a harbinger of things to come.

I waited. And I waited. Where the hell was Alvy? We had to get to our jobs! The minutes stretched thin, each headlight flashing down the block, a possible bus ride downtown.

Then, at last, Alvy came shuffling up the sidewalk, shoulders hunched as if the weight of Cleveland itself was strapped to his back. Even from twenty feet away, I could tell this wasn't just a late start. He was carrying something. Bad news has a gait of its own.

"Hey, Tommy." His voice cracked before my name was even finished.

"ALVY! Finally, man?" I said, relief ready to bubble over, but it turned sour when I saw his face.

"Um. Y'know, Tommy... um," said Alvy. And he paused, head down.

"WHAT!? What the hell, man! We missed the first bus! We're gonna be... Hey, was'a'matter?

"My dad says he won't never eat the sausage no more."

I looked at Alvy like he had three heads.

"What?!"

"And, and, we ain't even kosher, Tommy. I mean... he's a non-kosher Jew butcher who still won't eat the sausage!"

I laughed nervously, thinking he was pulling one of his weird Alvy jokes. "O... kay? The... sausage... then what?" I actually thought he was setting up a punchline.

But he wasn't joking. His eyes were steady, serious. He reached into something deeper than either of us had bargained for. "Um…'To everything there is a season, and a time for every purpose under heaven…'"

I felt my grin fall. "What'a'ya talkin' abou…"

He interrupted, "I, I, I ain't goin' to the station no more, Tom-bo. It, it ain't so groovy for me. Makes me feel, y'know, dirty—the kind you can't wash off. My dad says a man walks away from stuff like that." He gave a small shrug, and the shrug was worse than the words.

"I guess I seen how they make the sausage, too," he added quietly, but it hit me like a hammer.

My throat closed up. "Alvy, c'mon, it's… jus' showbiz." I wanted him to laugh and make it all fun again.

But he didn't. His mouth trembled, his voice steadied on scripture. "A, a, 'a time to keep, and a… a time to cast away,' Tommy."

Something in me just snapped. "See, that's why 'cuz you got held back in the fourth grade, you're such a tool!"

He flinched, but didn't back down. "Wha, 'what is crooked cannot be straightened, and what is lacking…'"

"NO! No, that's just your dumb religion, man! It's stupid! And, an'—if that's what your dad told ya, then he's a dum-dum, too!" The words left me before I could stop them, bitter and hot.

"SHUT UP!" His voice rose, fierce in a way I'd never heard from him. "He's a good man… and I decided this, Tommy, by my own self."

That one cut deeper than any insult. "No. NO! I, I, I can't believe this is you talkin', Alvy! THIS IS IMPORTANT TO ME!"

Another bus came down the street, brakes hissing, lights carving white onto the curb.

"I KNOW!" he burst. Alvy's eyes were wet, his fists clenched. "But… jus' not to ME!"

The bus doors swung open for my escape, my exit line. I charged toward it, tears burning, anger the only shield I had left.

"FINE! GREAT! Well, I'm GOIN'! And no one's gonna stop me! I love this, man! I LOVE IT, Alvy! And if you don't... Well, then... then you and me, we ain't never gonna be best friends no more. It's done!"

I climbed the steps and turned to fire a parting shot. "You! You're just a stupid Jew-idiot, Alvy! You know that?"

He didn't flinch this time. "Yeah, well, then you, you're a stupid, dago-wop idiot, then, too!"

I sat by the bus window, refusing to look out, though every muscle in my face screamed to look. The bus lurched, pulled away. I caught a sliver of him anyway—Alvy on the curb, shoulders shaking, sobbing, then walking off into the dark, alone.

And that was it. That was the end. Over. We never spoke again. Not in school. Not on the street. And I never got to apologize before he left for Vietnam, either. Damn it. I love him so. The bus took me forward... life took him away. And what was broken inside me that night stayed broken.

Back at the station, a recorded announcement blasted through the air with attention-grabbing sound effects and pulse-pounding music:

"The KYW request and dedication lines are OPEN! Call K-Y-Eleven-Hundred NOW for all of Mid-America!" the voice screamed.

VU meters danced wildly. Chick—calm as a surgeon and faster than one—cued up a 45-rpm and rode the volume knob with two fingers, a man at a tiny, holy organ.

The jingle singers tagged it with their bright jive:

We play what you say on hit-packed K-Y-W in Cleveland, Ohio!

Up comes "Baby, I Need Your Loving," a record so good even regrets stand up straighter when it plays.

Dicky, over the intro, pours on the microphone syrup:

"To Kitty, Kevin, Ed, Matt, and the gang at Parma High! Go Redmen! Happy first anniversary from Al to Suzanne in Toledo, aww. It's The Four Tops, sincerely yours, with their great ol' Negro spiritual…" and up came the first lyric. He'd hit the post perfectly.

In the Ansaphone studio, I watch through glass—a small fish bowl with a view of the big fish tank—and I felt my chest tighten.

They were all lies what Dicky said. All of 'em. I made up every one of those names 'cuz I was late. I dunno, maybe Alvy was right. I mean, it did seem wrong, lying to thousands of kids and all, but it really didn't hurt anyone, did it?

The heavy studio door opened on a cushion of silence—and Merk stepped in. His presence was like a weather front that lowers the temperature three degrees.

"Hey, was'sa matter? You all right?"

"Um, yeah… fine."

Merk looked at me like a teacher reading a note from Mom I'd forged with my wrong hand. "Yeah. I can see that. So, where's Shorty?"

"Um, I, I guess, Alvy… quit."

"Hm. Smart kid."

Merk nudged my shoulder, paused, and left. The thick door closed the way good doors do: decisively, like the end of a sentence you don't get to rewrite. And I sat alone. Thinking a lie is a thing you can carry and, sometimes, a thing that can carry you; but in this case, it did neither.

"Aw, it was just showbiz, right?" I rationalized, and God help me, I wanted… I needed to be part of it.

Have you ever heard the legend of "The Lady of the Lake"? When I was little, I remember seeing a picture book about her and King Arthur. I always thought she likely had a sister, one called Bessie, who lived in Lake Erie because I used to hear her shrill moaning blowing in over the water on frigid nights. This was one of those nights. I could feel the Lady breathe cold through her teeth outside, lean against the building, and listen to my pangs of guilt through brick and glass.

Inside KYW, everything else remained the same—transformers, tape carts, fluorescent lights. Just a congregation of people and electronics. But I thought if I was really sorry for my sin, maybe the Lady would absolve me. She didn't. She just listened, knowing the lie. The guilt I felt over made-up names sent out into the dark stung me to the core. But I decided at that moment that being part of the lies and illusion was better than being left outside of it. I had become a participating member of Radioland. And the night went on.

Dicky would keep reading Camus between breaks—a man hoping that a French philosopher had an answer for his and all of America's problems. Merk would keep counting pills like the warden of bedtime. Chick would slip tone arms onto giant transcriptions like a priest placing wafers on great tongues. And I—Tommy back then—would keep writing down names or making them up when time mocked me. Radio runs on the clock, the way the heart runs on blood, and sometimes you do whatever you can to do to keep the pulse.

Those nights still live with me. My bathroom miracle pee. Alvy's husky pants curse. Our never-resolved fight at the bus stop. The Faceless Black Manikin hovering impossibly eighteen stories up. That's the thing about radio, and gossip, and sin: sometimes the signal you send out is the one that returns to you, slightly delayed, distorted, but truer than true at the same time.

Only "The Lady in the Lake" knew the truth. And she would keep my secret.

SIX — "Bits and Pieces"

"Man is the only creature who refuses to be what he
is."— Albert Camus

A radio studio might be thought of as a
confident, bright space where true
performance artists steer their voices across
a dark sky like the predictable beam from a lighthouse.
Not that evening. The memory of that night still sends
chills, and I've spent countless years visualizing the
moment and piecing together what I think may have
happened with Dicky and me.

I now imagine the studio floating in strangeness,
a room taken hostage by a single, eerie bulb lit from
above. I could hear the Dave Clark Five beating time in
the background, but the music was muffled. The lyrics of
their hit, "Glad All Over," were indistinct. Just the bass
kicking and the snare tapping out an S-O-S in a Morse
Code only Dicky could decode.

Dicky was slouched in his chair at an angle
suggesting both defiance and defeat. He wasn't looking

at Chick in studio control, or at his notes, or even at me. He was staring past me, through me, toward a terrible visitor seated across from him—a Thing only he could see. The Faceless Black Manikin had returned. Dicky stared unflinchingly at its darkness. To me, it was just an empty chair. But the look of fear on Dicky's face told a different story. It's as if he was caught by surprise by a relentless pursuer. The Dave Clark Five's backbeat faded, and an uncanny silence enveloped.

I came in with the request slips, paper fanned like a deck of cheap cards, and stopped because something in Dicky's expression tightened the air. He dagger-eyed an invisible guest that demanded his attention. I set the papers on the console carefully and leaned in, trying to intercept his stare.

"Dicky? Y, you okay?"

His eyes flicked at me. He started to shudder. Not really a tremor in the usual sense. It was more of a quivering, like the way a tuning fork would vibrate.

"Um… Dicky?"

He turned back to the empty chair, and that's when it wasn't empty anymore—at least to him. The

Black Specter was up from its seat, hunched at Dicky's console, its arm stretching until its hand hovered inches from my face. I felt nothing, but Dicky sure felt it. He turned to me screaming:

"NO! GET THE FUCK OUT! NOW! GET OUT! RUN!"

His blast shook me to my ankles. I bolted, tears hot and instant. I hit the door with the force of panic and confusion, and I slammed into Merk in the hallway.

Behind me, I imagined the lights flashed back on, flooding the studio. Dicky's mind trick had ended, and the nightmare was gone. Radioland clattered back into place: the consoles, the cart racks, the glass to the booth, everything harmless in the brightness of reality.

Merk steadied me, but my tears had their own momentum. I cried loudly and uncontrollably.

"Jesus! Wha the hell's this now?" he barked.

In the studio, a click came from the intercom. "Comin' out in ten, Dick," Chick's voice filtered, and something in Dicky snapped him back to his radio self—his working self. He slid on his headphones with the calm of a man who couldn't remember he'd just lobbed a grenade. The music nudged up in the monitors. He pointed at the mic. The music ducked. An ON AIR sign went red.

"Ooo yeah, baby! Feelin' Gladys all over…"

He pointed again. Chick threw a cart. The sexy female drop-in voice oozed, "Ohhhhh! Mmmm."

"The far too handsy Dave Clark Five… and time for another…"

He cued Chick, who rolled in the tape reverb like a carnival mirror.

"K-Y, TWIN, (twin, twin!) SPIN, (spin, spin!)"

The next record skid-sparked to life—"Bits and Pieces," Dave Clark again. The mic clicked off, and oxygen reclaimed the room.

Just outside the studio, I was still on my knees, hysterical and confused. Merk stood by, clueless and furious in equal measure.

"What? Wha'd I do, Merk?" The question fell out of me with genuine vacancy, and something in Merk's eyes decided not to escalate the issue. He waved it off like a bad smell. Merk folded to one knee beside me and pulled out a handkerchief the size of a small picnic blanket—blue, soft, clean, as if he'd known I'd need it.

"Hey, hey, hey. 'At's all right, kid. Shh. It's okay, buddy. Here."

"I don't know what happened," I managed, small as a prayer.

"Yeah. Well, he don't either."

"But, I didn't do anyth...?"

"No, no. You did nothin'. He's done that shit to me, too. It, it ain't you, pal. See, Dicky's got a... " Merk twirled a finger at his temple in that universal mime for crossed wires. "Dicky gets... sad, all right? But, but I know he didn't mean nothin' by it. Okay? C'mon."

He hauled me up like he was lifting a muskie out of the lake, steadying my elbow and checking for leaks.

"You good?"

I nodded. Wiped my nose and blew a fairly substantial discharge into its center. Then tried to hand the hanky back.

"Um... Yeah, no... You keep it. Let's go. Back to work, huh?"

He slung an arm across my shoulders and we started down the hall, his stride helping my legs do what they wouldn't.

Back in the deejay booth a few minutes later, Merk held out a pill like a peace treaty. Dicky looked at it and then at Merk, with confusion on his face.

"I did? Really? Shit. I, I, can't remem...I, I'm... so sorry."

"Hey, don't sorry me. You owe that kid an apology. Here. This'll help." He pressed a pill into Dicky's palm, then barked when Dicky hesitated. "No, no! Take it! And no more'a your bullshit. C'mon! Let's go!"

Dicky took it like a man taking a dare, swallowed and grimaced. "Goddamn! I hate these things. Ech! I hate this whole fuckin' business."

"Aw, jeez. Here we go again," Merk muttered, the way a man mutters when he's heard a jukebox pick too many times.

I nudged the studio door open with a new handful of names. Just a crack, standing in the margin between visibility and silence, and I slid inside without announcing myself. Dicky didn't see me yet. He was already tumbling into the argument he'd kept cued up for days.

"No, no, no, Merk! Hear me out..."

"C'mon..." Merk said, exasperated.

"You wanna know why, huh? It's the noise, Merk. The the constant... pounding... s... sound comin' outta this room. Wave after wave of... mind-numbing... noise. And I'm part of the problem."

"So what?!"

"So, wha? Noise!" Dicky spread his arms wide. "It, it blocks people from focusin,' Merk, from, from thinkin.'"

"C'mon, who cares!? It's nothin'! S'entertainment! Little music, some jokes. Why not? Makes people feel less alone. What'sa matter with that?"

"Cuz... cuz we are alone, Merk. People need'a think about that."

"Oh, do they now!"

"Yeah, all of it. Life, death, meaning!"

"Meanin'!?" Merk scoffed. "Christ, people don't wanna think about hard shit they can't do nothin' about, and neither do I. Why worry? Eat, drink, and fuck Mary — pardon my French, kid," as he poked a finger at me.

I raised my eyebrows despite myself and clamped down on a grin. This was a conversation conducted at the edge of a cliff that had picked up speed.

Dicky lifted a slim book from a stack on the counter, its cover gray and stern. "You sound like what's called a nihilist, man."

"Yeah? Well, I don't know what that means," Merk said. "But if you're saying the world sucks ass, and it does, and that we're stuck in a place that no one asked if we wanted to be, and we are, then at least let's have a fuckin' party to make shit... suck less! If that's what's goin' on here, then, yeah, I'm one'a those what you said."

Dicky smiled with a kind of rue. "Okay, so you're a cheerful nihilist."

"Bullshit... I ain't never been cheerful." Merk tossed the line over his shoulder at me, then jerked his chin toward the door. "C'mon, kid! Out!"

I stepped forward first and set a few more request slips on Dicky's console like an offering.

"Hey, Tommy!" Dicky said. "We gotta talk later. I'm kind'a busy right now. Okay, pal?" I nodded, smiled, and let Merk herd me out.

But I looked back, just once, over my shoulder. He was still there—our prince of night music with book in hand, Albert Camus' *Reflections on the Guillotine*, as a commercial about ham and housewives played in the background.

That night, I learned something else about Dicky that you'd never guess by just listening... He sure read a lot of books! Yeah, the station was an ecosystem of contradictions: jokes painted over philosophical dread.

"Comin' out in fifteen, Pep," Chick said.

Dicky closed the book, nodded, and cocked a finger, timing his breath to the waning of the pre-recorded ad copy. Then he interacted behind, around, and in between the taped announcer's spiel. His snide was hilarious, well, to me.

"That's why a delicious slice of Krakus Polish ham really satisfies..." The recorded voice intoned with Sunday-dinner consequence.

"Oh, I bet," Dicky said in the little silences the copywriter had left for punctuation. He accompanied the line with an unmistakable, juvenile jerk-off hand motion. Chick, watching, turned red-faced, laughing. I was in the Ansaphone booth by then and still heard it—Chick's laugh cutting sharp through soundproof glass.

"Great in a sandwich or as a Sunday dish, you just can't beat it..." the voice promised, rich with authority.

"Well, not at the table," Dicky deadpanned, and Chick made a snorting noise from which he might never recover.

"So, get crackin' with delicious Krakus Polish hams today!"

Then Dicky honked his trumpet and said, "I'll tell ya this much. With a name like Krakus, it's gotta be Polish."

He pointed without looking. Chick fired the Sonovox: "Hubba-hubba!"

"Krakus Ham, for all your slapping pleasure. SHOPPING!" Dicky corrected, and Chick answered with the "Crazy Man" drop-in: "Oh, no! Noooooh!"

Dicky laughed. "Available at all Kroger deli departments!"

Another cue jab. The jingle rose like cream rising in coffee.

"You are lis-ten-ing to K-Y-W!..." the singers chimed in that hyper-bright advertising harmony that made you think the world might be fine if everyone would just clap on two and four.

"Stunner!" Dicky cut in, threading his voice into and throughout the harmonies.

"You are a Wild Child..." they promised.

He sang along on the next line, badly, delighted to vandalize the perfection.

"You gotta' lot'a cool! And you gotta' alot'a sass! You're alive! You're alert!..."

"You're not dead!" Dicky inserted

"You're a gas!"

"Ooo. Maybe too much Polish sausage!" He added, and again I could hear Chick howl.

"You are listening to K-Y-W! You got a mass of class!"

Right there, on the record's inhale, Dicky slid in like a shortstop: "It's your Swingin' Dicky on K-Y! Spincerely yours... Beatles!"

The needle dropped, and there it was: "Do You Want to Know a Secret," a song that made me think of my junior high schoolyard, and breath clouds, and girls with parkas zipped to their noses. And a difficult night for me, somehow grew softer at the edges. I could feel it.

Out front, Mom idled by the curb in our dented chariot, knitting by the faint dome light glow. Carmel was asleep in the back seat with her mouth open, a tiny stalactite of drool shining on her chin. Walter snored on her lap like a model of loyalty carved from warm bread. I jogged out after my shift and slid in.

"There he is!" Mom said.

Walter erupted, tail-propeller cutting the air as he bounded over the seat and licked at my neck with a wet blessing.

"Aw, shit. AGAIN!" Carmel groaned, surfacing from her impromptu nap.

"Carmel, SHUSH!" Mom snapped. "I will wash out your mouth with Cuyahoga River water. Swear to God! Oh, Where's Alvy?"

"B, bar mitzvah... uh, homework," I said, which was not really a lie, just not coordinated enough to be the truth.

We pulled away, the station shrinking in the rearview. Downtown's wet streets reflected stoplights, and the melting red and green Christmas ornaments the city still hadn't taken down. The radio inside the car droned KYW low, still scattering its signal into houses, factories, and bedrooms full of the lonesome.

At home, something wasn't right. The living room lights were on, and on our davenport, I saw the back of Dad's head. He was still in his work clothes, as if the mill had only loaned him out for the evening. He held a bottle of Duquesne beer in one hand and a cigarette in the other, the pose of a man who knows how to hold on to what little he has. The car nosed into the driveway and coughed and shook before Mom turned it off. We tumbled out with my hangover of radio adrenaline fading, the house welcoming us into warmth.

Mom, me, Walter—our small parade—moved up the stairs toward the living room. Carmel trailed in, eyes half-closed, with an odd, diagonal Howdy Doody-like trot.

"Vinny! You're home!" Mom sounded surprised and a little wary.

"Yeh. Bloomin' mill's down, sent us early. Where youse been this late?"

Walter launched himself across the room and leaped into Dad's lap, slathering his face with unconditional love.

"HO! Damn asshole-licker! No! Get the hell OFF!" Dad pushed Walter down with the flat of his forearm. I know he loved Walt and dogs in general, but right now, he was a guy who had only a certain number of tolerances, and they were all used up.

Carmel peeled in the living room. "I HATE radio," she said and collapsed, like a Huckleberry Hound cartoon, face-first into the couch next to Dad.

Uh-oh! I rolled my eyes. Mom drooped as if the strings holding her up had been cut with scissors. Dad stared—eyes narrowed, calculating the equation of who we were and who we were supposed to be.

"What... did she say?!"

"Aw, honey. Now, don't be mad," Mom said, sounding as if she was pushing a piano up the stairs with words.

"Emph. Too damn tired for mad." He sighed in resignation. "Eh! Youse jamokes, go! Bed! Now! S' late! School tomorrow! C'mon, c'mon!"

I looked at Mom for permission—her nod was a blessing. Carmel and I fled up the upstairs, Walt following with a penitent doggie's side-eye to Dad.

Mom lowered herself onto an ottoman near Dad, the kind of perch wives take when they have to explain something to a man who hates explanations. Dad drained the last line of his "Duke," set the bottle on the coffee table, and said, "All right. So? Why?"

"Our Tommy. He's... in love," she said. "It was the only way I knew how to... teach him."

"Mm-hm. How long doin' this back 'n' forth?"

"Just 'bout a... month or so."

Dad squinted into the kitchen, shook his tired head, and sighed. "Yeah. You, um, you ain't helpin' me out here, Adelaide."

He got up, heavy with worry, and shuffled toward the pantry, the cigarette pointing the way, a small light that could only warn of rocks already hit.

Upstairs, I sat on the edge of my bed and watched Walter circle three times before accepting the rug's hospitality. My slightly open bedroom window poured the sound of our neighbor's TV laugh track from the alley. I could still hear the ghost of the studio in my ears: Chick's muffled cackling, the spin of carts, Dicky's voice coasting in that sweet spot between mischief and melancholy.

Here's what I know now, and maybe I knew then, but didn't say out loud: radio WAS noise and it wasn't. Dicky railed against noise, but he was the same guy with his face in Camus, trying to thread a needle between absurd despair and his duty during a frickin' ham commercial. He said people were alone and needed to recognize that. Merk said people were alone and needed to not to be. I was almost thirteen and thought that maybe both arguments should hold hands long enough for me to fall asleep.

Back downstairs, the conversation went on without me. It would be decided, as things always are, by the weight of habit and the torque of love.

But in that studio, under that unforgiving bulb and Dicky's startling outburst, something had shifted inside me. A man had seen a Faceless shape and shouted to protect me from it, with the urgency of someone trying to save a boy from a train that only he could hear. Then his mind cleared, and he turned the show back on. He made a dirty joke about Krakus ham and got the Sonovox to purr. He sang badly over a jingle and then handed off the night to the Beatles.

Earlier that evening, when I'd watched him clutch *Reflections on the Guillotine*—Camus' story about the absurd morality of power seeking justice by killing someone regardless of their crime—I saw it plainly: Dicky read not to escape but to hold onto a railing in a crazy house without stairs. The Faceless

Black Manikin was probably his only fear. But he felt it was real enough and near enough to scream a warning to me. I don't know, really. I've replayed that night so many times that the tape has a worn spot. The music, the shout that made me run, the grown men in their argument about life's meaning. You could easily dismiss it all and just say Dicky was fucked up by pills, or booze, or the stress of choosing a nomad's life in an unforgiving, money-driven corporate world. That was part of it, I suppose.

I was a kid, yes. But that night felt like the first time I understood grown-ups as troubled travelers boarding the same late bus, hoping that someone, anyone, knew the route. Dicky with his Camus. Merk with his party-or-die pragmatism. And me, old enough to hold two ideas at once and young enough to think I was onto something.

The Beatles sang,"Do You Want to Know a Secret," to a city like it could keep one. The night did what nights do: it went on. The mill may or may not fire up in the morning. Chick would cue the jingle; Merk would find new ways to call bullshit and mean, "I love

171

you." And somewhere in those pages by Camus—about justice and how to live with knowledge you can't unknow—Dicky would find a sentence that would catch in his mind and make him choose, again, to go back on the air.

I kept Merk's handkerchief like a relic, folded in my pocket until it fell apart into blue confetti. If you've ever been a child who ran because a man you loved screamed at you, you keep things. You keep the song titles, too—"Glad All Over," and "Bits and Pieces"—like street names you can still find your way by when all the roadway signs go missing.

And the jingles? Jingles were my liturgy. They promised that you were alive and alert, and though Dicky couldn't resist the gag—"You're not dead!"—the fact was, we weren't. Not yet. Not that night. We were breathing in sync with the tower, matching our pulses to its soft red blink. "You are listening to K-Y-W," the jinglers sang. Sometimes, in my head, I still am.

Downstairs, a chair scraped tile. A fresh bottle of beer church-keyed open. Voices lowered the way voices do when truth is about to enter the room. Mom said something I didn't catch. Dad's answer was slower, but I knew the cadence: a man finally making room for me and my dreams—a child he'd somehow raised without a manual. It sounded like permission with conditions, like love, rust-belt style—less a valentine, more a union contract.

I lay back on the bed, and the ceiling swam its old, faithful constellations of hairline cracks. The next day would bring whatever it brought—more noise, more meaning, more chores. But for a few hours, the night gripped our small, funny family close and held in its palm a radio show that was braver than it knew how to admit.

I didn't fall asleep fast. No one could after a night like that. But eventually, the city's drone of faraway sirens and the background of white noise traffic stitched itself to my wandering mind and pulled me under. And I went, gratefully, still holding the thread of Merk's kindness in my fist like a kid who had finally learned that you can walk a dark corridor, so long as somebody's at the other end showing you the way.

"Spincerely yours, Merk." Tommy.

Seven — The Manikin

"Battle not with monsters, lest ye become a monster; and
if you gaze into the abyss, the abyss gazes also into
you."
— Friedrich Nietzsche

N ow, here's where the world tilts, the part
where station gossip got way too real. What
came next was straight from the darkest
corners of Dicky's skull, where the Faceless Black
Manikin never left. But later, I heard all about it. A little
from Merk, a bit from Chick's grapevine, and later a
whole lot from tater stories in *The Cleveland Press*.
Here's what I pieced together, or maybe dreamed up. I
really can't say.

From Dicky's apartment balcony, eighteen floors
up, Lake Erie's dark horizon lay before him in cold, wet
armor, a seam that had been ironed flat. From his outside
deck, the wind had a biting, mineral smell, a wet knife
against the gums. He was hunched over the balcony
guardrail, hair standing in nervous peaks, eyes veined

and watery with the red itch of a long, bad night. He held a paperback with both hands like a life preserver—*The Stranger*, a novella Camus penned about an outsider confronting the nearness and certainty of death. His lips moved as he read; you could see him trying to climb the grim sentences, rung by rung. Then, halfway up, the ladder wobbled.

Dicky paused, his thumb holding the page, and the ideas between two sentences became too wide to cross. His tears exploded, fast and convulsive, with no prelude, no dignity. The first broken sob dragged the rest after it, and he folded, shoulders shaking, face wet, a grown man with a child's helplessness pouring out of him.

The book slipped. He didn't throw it. His hands simply let go. The rectangle tumbled past seventeen balconies, a small falling truth against an indifferent blue-black night sky. The Lady in the Lake didn't blink. The horizon didn't raise an eyebrow. Cleveland's distant city lights glowed indifferently off to the right.

Dicky heaved in tears and tipped a bourbon bottle to his mouth. The swallow burned, but he took another hit. Then he shouldered through the sliding door and staggered into his apartment, bumping the frame, the Jim Beam bottle clacking off the jamb.

Inside, the living room was the kind of mess that forms around a single man's loneliness: records in teetering stacks, magazines loosened from their bindings, and an ashtray overflowing with Rhonda's recent lipstick stains. And there, in a chair opposite the couch, sat the Faceless Black Manikin. It chose a casual sprawl, legs out, elbows on thighs, a parody of a friend who dropped by and intended to stay. Its head—featureless—tilted toward Dicky with an attention that felt like ridicule. And the Thing pointed at him.

Dicky stopped and backed away as his spine found the wall, pressed flat against the chalky plasterboard. The sight (and "sight" is the wrong word; you can't see a phantom, but you feel it seeing you) struck him full in the chest. The bourbon bottle sweated in his grip; his fingers were unreliable, wet with their own heat. CRASH. The bottle slipped from his hand and shattered on the hardwood; its amber bled toward the rug in branching rivers.

Then a sound. That sixty-kilocycle tone uncoiled again in his mind, thin and metallic. The noise started quietly, then sharpened and drilled his teeth and the bone behind his eyes. It grew more shrill until his head buzzed like a chainsaw. Dicky clapped both palms over his ears, a child's defense against thunder. But the shrill was already inside, a wire heated white, a bright, burning filament. The Manikin did not move. It didn't have to. It kept its finger out, waiting and staring without eyes. Something in Dicky's throat snapped.

"NO! GO AWAAAY!"

It came out of him ragged and raw, a strip torn off his voice. The walls were not actually moving, but they decided to make him think they were. They leaned in by a hair and came closer, then squeezed closer still, like a tightening vice. He braced his feet and pushed with his shoulders as a fever rose behind his eyes. The Manikin's gesture didn't change; the tilted head and the long finger still found their target.

Dicky took aim at the only surface that would yield and slammed his forehead into the drywall. Once. Twice. The sound was hollow, a cheap drum. Plaster dust lifted in a small, uncelebrated storm. On the third blow, a crack spidered the wall; on the fourth, Dicky's skin split, and blood drew a proof line down his temple. The tone drilled louder—then stopped and fell away in a sudden collapse. Dicky was left trembling in a room that seemed to reclaim its ordinary sounds—the hum of the refrigerator motor, a heat pipe ticking as it cooled.

But the Manikin hadn't vanished. Of course, it hadn't. It sat with the unmoving attention of a mantis. When it spoke, the words weren't in the room. They came from somewhere else, threading past where sound should have been.

Noise, it said. That's all you are.

Dicky's mouth worked; the denial stumbled out sideways. "No."

A tilt of its blank head and the suggestion of a smile that didn't require a mouth. You hide in the noise. And when it ends, you hear me. Let's… make it stop.

Dicky shook his head hard. The bourbon on his breath turned to shame. He tried to breathe the word "pointless" but found it absurd in his mouth.

Sobbing, Dicky pushed off the wall and lurched down the hallway to the bedroom. He yanked open the closet and got a whiff of cardboard, leather belts, and old coats. Dicky grabbed at boxes with the blind fury of a man who already knows what he's looking for and hates himself for it. Shirts slumped to the floor. A clot of wire hangers rattled. He tugged the pull chain, and the closet bulb clicked on with a bruise of yellow light.

Behind him stood the Manikin "watching." It cocked its head to the left as Dicky pulled out one box and flung another behind him. That's when the Thing stood stick straight. Dicky seized a hidden hatbox. The weight of it told him the truth. It was shoved way in the back to be used in emergencies only. Dicky unwrapped it on his bed with careful, but shaking hands. A handgun. Dull, discreet, something that had been waiting for its name to be called.

Good, the Manikin murmured.

Dicky didn't answer. There's a point where language stops being useful, and the gun would speak soon enough.

Back in the living room, Dicky lowered himself onto the couch slowly, deliberately. He set the gun across his knees and looked at it as if it might offer some comforting counsel. In the silence, he snapped open the cylinder and tipped it. Gunpowder-filled brass spilled into his lap.

Across from him, the Manikin reclaimed the chair. It arranged itself with theatrical ease, hands on its legs with a posture of anticipation. The time had arrived. Dicky lifted his head and stared into the Thing's void where a face should be. He felt seen, judged, and discarded all at once.

"Can't you jus' LEAVE ME ALONE!" He shouted, not caring what the neighbors across the thin walls thought.

The Manikin didn't bother to reply. It lifted one finger and aimed it at the bullets in his lap, the way a teacher points at a chalk mark and waits for a student to put two and two together.

Dicky shook his head, a small, involuntary refusal. His face contorted in tears. "No. P, p, please."

When Dicky looked back up, the Black Enigma had extended his entire arm in a point. Dicky obeyed as if hypnotized. He plucked out a single round. The brass was cool as he slid it into the chamber, spun the cylinder, and placed the muzzle in his mouth. There was no thought, no prayer, no pause. The click was clean, mechanical, obscene in its confidence. A pause. Then another resigned CLICK! Again, tears slid down his cheeks.

The Manikin leaned back with folded arms, as if satisfied.

The Thing breathed. Once more. Dicky closed his eyes, hoping darkness would strip the words of their power. He knew those words came from inside his fractured mind, where all the worst voices keep their dark dreams.

Dicky whispered, "Once more."

Just then, in the hallway outside, an elevator dinged with hotel politeness. Merk's footsteps were softened by the old carpet as he approached the door. A knuckle rapped hard once, then continued in a steady tattoo.

"DICKY! C'mon! Open up, man!"

BLAM! A single shot cracked like a plate. Merk jerked to alarm. "HO! SHIT! DICK! HEY!" Fists pounded wood. The doorknob rattled. Merk reached for the apartment keys, fumbling. Metal kissed metal in the poor coordination of panic and love, fighting for control. "Christ Jesus!"

The lock turned, and the door swung wide. Merk's eyes flicked across everything in a snap: the spilled bourbon, the crooked, blood-dried comma on Dicky's brow, and the gun still loose in his grip.

"You ruined it, Merk. You ruined it." Dicky's voice was low and hoarse, all gravel and ash. There wasn't hatred in it, not even anger. It was something closer to shock and grief's unflattering cousin: shame.

Merk's throat clenched, fighting against his impulse to shout, but he made his voice small and steady. "Hey, hey, hey!" He took a single step in, palms open, as if he was approaching a skittish animal he didn't want to spook.

Dicky glanced down at his own hand, surprised to find the gun still attached to it. Confusion flickered—"Oh, God."—and he let it go. The thing hit the floor. Then he collapsed forward, arms around Merk, grasping like a drowning man. The sobs came back, ugly and useless. They emptied him.

Merk closed both arms around him and took the weight. He guided Dicky two small steps away from the gun with the easy authority of a man who'd shepherded drunks and foolish friends through worse nights than this.

"Okay, it's all right, kid. It's over. Shh. It's okay now. Shh," Merk said. He hugged Dicky tight, clasping Dicky's face in both his hands.

"Here, here, look'a me. I'm here now. I'm with ya, man," Merk said, feeling Dicky's temple cut sticky under his palm, and the stink of fresh black powder still sharp in the room. And Merk kept on talking because sometimes talking is the only way to reestablish reality.

"It's done, Dicky. Nothing can hurt you now, pal."

After a pause, in a moment of clarity, Dicky pulled away.

"Don't tell Ken. Please. Not Ken. Promise me ya won't, Merk."

The words arrived hot and desperate. In another room, in another world, that plea might have sounded petty. In this room, it was survival. Ken was consequences and ledgers; Ken was judgment that kept human pain as a spreadsheet line item. Dicky was asking to be spared a second trial while the first verdict still rang in his ears.

Merk breathed heavily and dragged Dicky to a chair. If he saw the Manikin, he gave no sign. If he didn't, it didn't matter. The shape of it sat in the room anyway when Dicky looked, then folded away like smoke.

Merk tightened his arms and let the promise he was about to make anchor him to the floor.

"Sure, sure. Yeah, yeah, yeah. No one's gotta know, pal. This is between us, okay? Just take a deep breath, all right? We're gonna get'cha some help, Dick, I'm here now. I got'cha. I got'cha, man."

KYW's executive offices smelled as if old carbon paper had seeped into the woodwork. Even in "Top Management" you could still hear the air studio thumping bass notes through the floors. Program director Ken Apati sat behind his desk, shirt collar open and tie skewed like it had given up halfway through strangling him. His desk blotter had burn marks from cigarettes stubbed out in a hurry. A space charred by impatience.

"He did WHAT!?" Ken demanded.

"Yeh. I checked him into Fairhill this mornin'. Dicky's... really sick, man."

"Again!? That goddamn prick! Look, we're payin' you sixty-five a week to make sure shit like this doesn't happen!" Ken's voice carried like gravel. "Christ, if the press finds out, we're fucked royal! Have you been feedin' him the pills?"

Merk stood across from him, a little hunched, guilty like a boy dragged to the principal's office. He rubbed at the crease in his slacks with his thumb and nodded. "Yeah! Sure! All'a time, jus' like you said. But they ain't helpin'. I, I think he's shell-shocked or somethin'."

Ken leaned forward, eyes bright with contempt. "Nah. He's a goddamn freak! A loner! A LOSER! The station he came from in Erie, TOLD me he'd be a fuckin' problem. Should'a never hired the asshole."

"Ken. C'mon, Dicky's great."

"He's acting out… like a fuckin' child."

"No. It's like some kind'a nervous breakdown, I tell ya. Like, like a, a spell he gets." Merk's tone softened, nearly pleading. "He… thinks too much, y'know. He's… lost, depressed."

"Depressed?" Ken sneered, spitting the word like poison. "Yeah, well, so am I, Merk, so's half the goddamn country. Eh, take a fuckin' Miltown, grow some balls, and deal with it."

"Whoa, a lil' compassion, eh?" Merk stepped back, stung.

"Hey, I got compassion runnin' out my crack for real sick people." Ken sat back, exhaled hard, grabbed a pack of Lucky Strikes, and lit up. "But the drama with this shitheel! Jesus! Up one day, down the next? I know the type."

Merk, quieter now: "So, um... what we gonna do?"

"Kick his precious ass to the curb if I could. But, we're still in these goddamn ratings. FUCK!" Ken slammed his fist down on the desk. His anger ran through the room like a thunderclap.

Silence followed. Fluorescent lights buzzed. Merk shifted on his feet, hands hanging uselessly. He was loyal, but loyalty's a fragile currency when the boss wants blood.

"All right." Ken growled, "So, I'll cover for him today and over the weekend. That's three days to get his shit together. But if he's not back on the air Monday night... Dicky's finished. And you ain't lookin' too good, either."

"Now, why you gotta go there, huh?" Merk bristled. He'd take a lot, but not the suggestion that his own hide was in the pot.

"Hey, I'm just sayin' it's an easy gig for ya, Merk."

"Phfft. I ain't so sure 'bout that."

"Better 'an goin' back sellin' on the street, man, and right now you're blowin' it."

Merk's shoulders stiffened. He didn't need that reminder. "All right! Fine! I'll... take care of it."

"Oh, wait. Here!" Ken dug in a drawer, pulled out two small bottles rubber-banded together, and tossed them across the desk. They clattered once before Merk caught them. Inside, the uppers and downers clinked like hailstones. "Another week's supply, blues and reds. Shove 'em down his fuckin' throat if you have to."

Merk nodded, turned, hand on the doorknob, then hesitated. His voice was careful, like stepping on thin ice. "Not for nothin', but ah, how you scorin' these things?"

Ken didn't flinch. "Knowls. Juggy. That, ah, that... record promoter. Ya know'im?"

Merk let out a low breath. "Juggy. Yeah. Yeah, I do."

"Three days, Merk! Three!" Ken barked, jabbing his fingers into the air like a curse.

Merk exited, leaving Ken alone with his cigarette, his temper, and a station balanced on the back of one very sick man.

Ken picked up the office phone, dialed, and muttered into the receiver, "Sonofabitch."

At least, that's how Merk and the others told me it happened.

After hearing the full story and knowing what I now know, I thought back on the night Dicky blew up at me. I replayed the whole scene in my mind. I guess I did see something odd in his behavior. I recalled the music was boppin', the jokes were fast and crackin'. I was just the "request boy" outside the booth, watching a guy wrestle an invisible monster through glass thicker than my courage. But I remember the way Dicky's shoulders hunched, how his lips moved when no mic was hot. Later, after Merk told me the full tale, all the pieces fit together. I realized that Dicky wasn't fighting for the ratings or for his job. He was fighting for something precious. Fighting to keep his mind from being stolen by a Faceless void that wanted nothing more than to swallow him whole.

I now understood that the studio was Dicky's coffin with a microphone. I sensed that it took some real courage to sit in there for four hours. In studio control, Chick shuffled carts, trying to act oblivious to the man in a glass cage talking to no one. Merk watched, too, arms folded, jaw tight. They both thought the worst had passed — just another one of Dicky's "fits"—then another pill and another storm blown over. But Dicky knew the Manikin wasn't gone. It had just stepped back to catch its breath.

I remember that Dicky didn't flinch that night when me and the Faceless Black Thing dropped in—but I know he felt it sit down. He felt the absence of a face turning toward him; he felt the air turn colder, just as I had.

You know what I want, the Manikin must have said without moving lips it didn't have.

"Fuck you," Dicky whispered, barely audible even to himself.

Louder, it insisted. Say it. Make them all hear the filth inside you.

And what if he had? What if he said into his mic, "FUCK YOU PEOPLE! Fuck you ALL! Can't you see?! You kids are wastin' your life with this shit! Read a fucking book, you goddamn imbeciles! THINK!"? What if he broadcast that into the dark of Cleveland and beyond, letting the whole country hear him break apart live on air? A million ears would have turned to static because Swingin' Dicky Peppers finally swung his bat too hard.

The Dave Clark Five pounded through the monitors, cheerful and merciless. "I go to pieces! Bits and Pieces," every note a hammer in his skull.

The Manikin leaned close enough for him to smell its nothingness. Noise. Say it?

The Manikin's hands—black shapes, not quite solid—could have slid along Dicky's shoulders. Not weight, but pressure. Not touch, but intent.

Turn it off… forever, it cooed.

Then Dicky saw me standing there, request slips in my hand, and stopped because something in Dicky's expression tightened the air. He dagger-eyed the invisible Thing, grasping at me when I set the papers on the desk and leaned in, trying to intercept his stare.

"Dicky? Y, you okay?"

His eyes flicked at me.

"Um… Dicky?"

"NO! GET THE FUCK OUT! GET OUT! NOW! RUN!"

Yeah, I'm pretty sure that's what I saw—and didn't see—that night. Dicky's outburst was meant to save me and nothing else.

Anyway, that strange night bled on. Pills downed like Tic Tacs, Camus read like scripture, and jokes thrown like knives just to prove Dicky's hands weren't shaking. But the Falceless Black Manikin just sat somewhere nearby and waited, popping in and out of Dicky's tortured mind. It didn't scream. It didn't rush him. It whispered. It offered relief. And every time he flipped a record, every time he cued a cart, every time Chick laughed from across the glass, Dicky fought it.

Me? I cried in the hallway, then sat in the shadows of the request booth, too young to help, not old enough to understand. I saw a man battling a Faceless Thing that wanted him, a specter he couldn't escape. And though I didn't know the word for it then, I know it now: despair.

Eight — Dead Air

"You do not listen to silence; silence listens to you." —
Unattributed Zen saying

Fairhill Hospital's "specialty"was diseases of the mind. It carried a polished brightness that wasn't comfort so much as theater lighting, the kind that flattened shadows and insisted you look at what you didn't want to see. They said the place had been a Marine sanatorium once upon a time, but by the sixties, it was an "open" psychiatric facility—no locked doors, cheerful interiors, and early discharges. The brochures bragged about innovative therapies, but whispers said they fiddled with your soul.

Dicky went in on a Friday morning in a misty drizzle. The admitting nurse had a varnished smile and a rubber stamp that she thudded like a rubber gavel. Merk handled all the paperwork, then hung around to be with Dicky afterward. People didn't talk much about mental illness back then, not in our neighborhood, not anywhere, really. They called it "nerves" or "a spell."

They said, "he needs a rest," as if you could nap your way out of a hungry black ocean.

Merk told me all about it later—at least what he saw of it from the hallway as he peeked past the slightly open curtains in the "procedure room."

They rolled Dicky on a gurney with the slow dignity of a parade float that had lost its marching band. A gauze patch sat crooked on his forehead, where sanitized tape held the wound he had given himself. The room was trimmed in white and chrome, glass-clean, and cool like the inside of a refrigerator. Fluorescent tubes hummed. Everything had a lid, a latch, a dial. The air smelled of disinfectant.

Dicky turned his head and must have seen it, the Faceless Black Manikin, that mind-thing that stared back, always with him, framed in the doorway, just a smear in his peripheral vision. Merk knew Dicky had seen something because he flinched, turned away, and blinked hard. When he looked back, the Thing—never but always there—was gone. And, Dicky calmed down.

At the foot of the rolling bed stood the doctor: Harold Mendel, fifties, a man arranged in angles—thin, square jaw, square shoulders, square decisions. He had the precise hands of someone who believed in the instrument he was about to use. And the kind eyes of someone who'd learned the limits of such belief.

On Dicky's right was Nurse Pauline, thirties, the one with the clear gel. She moved with a speed that never looked rushed, the kind of professional competence you only notice afterward. She squeezed the conductive goo on his temples, careful to avoid Dicky's wound, then positioned the electrodes with the tidy poise of a person setting teacups.

"Okay, Richard. This is so you won't bite through your tongue or break teeth, all right?" Pauline said gently, but not tentatively.

She positioned the hard rubber guard in his mouth, firm and practiced. A small, almost mothering pat to the corner of his mouth.

"There we go. Comfortable?"

Dicky nodded in concession. Pauline tipped her chin toward Mendel, who gave a small nod back, the kind of permission that swung the next hinge.

On the other side stood Nurse Lila, late twenties, with freckles that made her seem younger until she spoke. Lila was the dose and the countdown. She stepped in with the hypodermic and found the line in his arm.

"Okay, hun, this'll relax you a bit, all right? Listen as I count back from ten. Look here. I'm gonna count, all right? Let's count together. Here we go now. Ten..." Lila said, voice paced like a metronome.

Dicky nodded again. The needle emptied; a coolness spread up his arm and hand like frost.

"...nine, eight, seven..." they said—Lila and Dicky—like a lullaby with the sugar burned off, and Dicky "relaxed."

Two assistants had already tightened the leather straps around his arms and legs. Artie, thirty, compact, and soft-spoken, the kind of guy who seemed too timid to be in this business. Stan, also thirty, broad-shouldered, with the patient strength of a man who knows not to lift with his back. They placed their gloved hands lightly on Dicky's shoulders and ankles, a secular scene that looked like a prayer circle.

Mendel touched a dial with reverence. "Fifty joules for five seconds. Ready?" He said, his gaze flicking to each of them—the ritual check, the tiny ceremony of consent within a room where consent had narrow corridors.

Everyone nodded. Pauline's thumb rested near the electrodes. Lila had her eyes on the second hand of her watch. Artie watched Dicky's face, reading it like a chart. Stan angled his body between bed and cart, a fence against the unpredictable.

"And... administer," Mendel said.

The unit made a crack, like a held breath turning into a snapped wire. The current zapped Dicky's brain, invisible as air, absolute as a commandment. His chest heaved once, his feet shot forward in a helpless arc, and he shook wildly. For a moment, his body was fully electrolyzed—everything working as planned, yet the outcome was unpredictable. Dicky's jaw clenched around the rubber for five seconds that seemed like an eternity. Then the machine went still. Mendel watched the needle return to zero. And it was over.

They loosened the straps, not all the way—nothing at Fairhill went all the way—and waited. Artie smoothed the sheet, which felt like an apology for what the sheet had just witnessed. Dicky's eyes fluttered beneath his lids like tiny moths. Pauline wiped the gel, brisk and kind. Lila wrote short notes, her pencil writing what no one wanted to say aloud. Mendel stood with his palm flat on the rail, as if making contact reassured them both.

No one said, "Good job." Who would you say it to?

Later that afternoon, in weather that couldn't decide between clouds and cold rain, Merk stood at the curb just outside the KYW building, working a cigarette. Ken had given him a couple of small pill bottles earlier—Juggy's weekly fix for Dicky—and Merk turned them in his palm, considering them with a look that was part disgust, part contempt, then tossed both bottles into an outdoor trash can. I heard him say, "Fuck this shit," as I walked up from my usual bus ride.

That's when Merk told me Dicky was sick, so we had the night off and that we needed to talk. Uh-oh. The way he said "talk" sounded like some of the pow-wows I had with my Dad, and my stomach turned a bit.

We walked—fists in our pockets, down toward the old Hannah Theater to Otto Moser's bar, this really cool joint where all the big shots from local TV, newspapers, and radio hung out.

Inside, the place smelled of vinegar fries, varnish, and cigarette smoke; the tabletops were scarred with the initials of theatrical legends who'd once played in Cleveland's theater district. Waitresses threaded between chairs with precise choreography. Somebody had chalked the day's soup on a blackboard—Minestrone—in confident handwriting.

Merk ordered a beer and didn't look at the menu. I ordered a burger and fries because, to me, that's what a person in a movie would order when they wanted to seem older. In a while, a waitress set down the plates before me, Merk's beer, and two cloth napkins folded on the diagonal, which I thought was super classy.

It was all very "grown up" for a kid. It made me feel like I was finally in the club. Part of something grand and so much bigger and more important than me.

Merk drank, and I munched on the burger, picked at the fries, and watched the bar—mirrors, whiskey bottles, a row of men in sleeves rolled to the elbow, collars a little wilted, voices in a pleasantly low cloud.

Then Merk asked a question that still puzzles me. I guess, after having watched Dicky's earlier "procedure," he couldn't understand why anyone would want to work in broadcasting.

"So, why? Why do you do it, kid? I mean, why come to the goddamn station every night? There ain't nothin' in it for you."

I was ready for that one. "No! There is! It's cuz... radio, Merk! It's... the best! And I'm gonna be a deejay, too, someday. I, I wanna be just like Dicky!"

He squinted at me, the corners of his eyes crinkling, not with amusement but with a kind of questioned interest. "Oh, do you now?"

"Yeah! What a great life! I mean, who wouldn't?"

Merk shook his head, put the glass down, the base clicking wood. He looked at me long enough for the room noise to fade. Then he stood, fished a few bills from his pocket, and dropped them on the table.

"C'mon. I need'a show you somethin'."
I stood up so quickly that my knee bumped the table. Then we moved toward the front, and as we did, a sound rose from the bar, a chant with a meter to it.

"Jug-gy! Jug-gy! Jug-gy!" The bar patrons yelled in time—about six of them—pounding their fists on a longish table. Beer vibrated in glasses; full ashtrays jumped on the wood.

A heavyset guy with a moon-pink face and hair like a pad of steel wool—Juggy Knowls—carried several mugs toward the six-top like a prizefighter presenting championship belts. He had the stage smile of a man who thinks he's a big shot, and the only reason every Top 40 song he pushed became a hit.

Merk tugged at the door handle, then stopped, a muscle in his cheek flicking like a signal light.

"Wait. Hold up a sec," he said to me without looking. Then he walked toward Juggy with his arms half out, a sneaky grin across his face like the Joker in Batman comics.

"HO! Look'a what the pussy dragged in, boys!" Juggy called, the bar answering with laughter that had no warmth.

Merk closed the distance, feigning happiness, his grin unwavering, hands rising for a hug as if the room would applaud his good sportsmanship.

"Well, well. Mister Juggy Knowls in the flesh!"

The smile dropped as Merk drove his foot into Juggy's groin with the fierce economy of a man who had replayed this move for a hundred evenings. Juggy's face opened like a surprised fish! He folded, mugs flying, beer arcing in the air, descending like amber rain.

"THAT'S for Dicky Peppers, ya fuck!" Merk barked, finger stabbing the air at the man on his knees.

Other hands reached for Merk from every angle—threatening, restraining, grasping—he batted them away like gnats, shoulders ducking, hips setting, his body the memory of a guy who'd learned to survive unfriendly situations. He turned to me, already moving.

"Let's go. GO! GO! GO!"

"Who was...?" I started.

"C'mon! MOVE!"

We were out the door before the room finished deciding what had happened. Merk's face shone with a dampness that wasn't exactly perspiration, something more like aftermath. He fumbled for his car keys, found them, and we hit the darkening street where neon signs began their nightly rehearsal.

We drove east, wipers stuttering against a windshield that couldn't decide whether to fog up or drool with inside sweat. The city rolled by in strips: storefronts blinking, bus stops holding wet riders under silver domes of rain. Merk didn't talk. I didn't either.

Fairhill Hospital loomed before us, its façade cleaned into submission—cheery enough to win a photo in the paper, institutional enough to make your shoulders climb toward your ears. A sign out front offered arrows pointing this way and that, not directions but the illusion of directions.

Merk pulled in, parked, and set the gear with a motion that said he wished the car itself could make a different choice. We walked inside, and the floor echoed our steps. It felt foreign to me and a bit dangerous.

A nurse with professional warmth—I didn't catch her name, about fifty, brunette hair pinned into obedience—met us with a smile that had been sanded by years of telling visitors bad news.

"Let's walk, shall we? We'll go this way," she said, inflecting the words like a kindness. She led us down a corridor with windows that offered the gray of late midday and into a long white room—white walls, white floor, white ceiling, even the chairs had white tubular bones.

The patients in there were arranged along the perimeter. It reminded me of boats moored for winter. Some slept sitting up, the chin-to-sternum sleep that means your mind has left the dock. Some argued with the walls as if the paint would eventually answer. At a card table, two men leaned over checkers and moved pieces with the slow, ceremonious care of monks.

That's when I noticed her: the woman with the ball. Evelyn, "Evie," I heard the nurse call her. Evie, maybe early forties, hair in a practical bob that someone had recently chosen for her, navy cardigan buttoned wrong at the top. She paced forward, bounced a rubber ball once, caught it, pivoted, paced back, bounced, and caught it again. The bounce developed a rhythm of its own, a tick-tock of time that only she could hear. Her face was handsome in a stern way; maybe she was once a schoolteacher, I thought. Except for the eyes—those gave her away. They were bright but without cheer, like a flashlight finding corners. A smudge of chalk, or perhaps a bit of today's lunch, clung to her sleeve.

She turned mid-lap and locked eyes with me. Her gaze didn't ask, it assessed, as if measuring me for a new pair of pants. She offered me the ball with a small lift of her hand—an invitation to play or a test, maybe? I couldn't tell. I shook my head politely and looked away quickly, heat creeping to my cheeks. After a beat, she reclaimed her rhythm, and her quiet ritual resumed. To herself, not to me, she hummed a tiny tune between closed lips—four notes up, two down—the kind of melody you might use to walk children back from recess. She never spoke a word.

The nurse who brought us in touched my elbow, insistent, but not rough, and we crossed to Dicky. He sat in a wheelchair angled toward a window that framed a stand of trees, the afternoon light cinching itself to the narrow copse. His eyes seemed lit from behind by a dim filament, his smile had gone slack at the corners of his mouth. He looked like a man whose station had gone off the air but who kept announcing anyway.

"Hey, Dicky-boy. How ya doin', kid?" Merk said, in a voice of borrowed brightness.

After several beats, Dicky said, "Great... It's... nice."

"Hey! Look who I brought to cheer you up."

His pupils drifted, then found focus. "Oh, hey... Merk."

"Hey, buddy. You 'member lil' Tommy, here, don'tcha? From the station?" Merk's tone tipped upward at the end.

Dicky stared blankly at me. "I... I like it here." He said, answering a question no one had asked.

Behind us, Evie bounced and caught, bounced and caught, and the sound began to feel like a code. I took a step closer, searching Dicky's face for his famous mischief, the guy who could make Cleveland feel like the center of the world.

"Dicky. No offense, but... how can you like it here?" I heard my own voice and didn't recognize it—thin, a string twanged too tight.

His smile made me shiver. "Dead air," he said slowly in a hush that wasn't peace.

That tore something in me I'd thought was knotted and tied double. In a studio, dead air is the catastrophe, the sin that gives managers and engineers ulcers. Here, it was a verdict pronounced so gently you could almost thank the judge.

For a second, I thought I saw the Black Manikin again, just over Dicky's shoulder—loneliness shaped like a man without features—but when I blinked, it was only a reflection of the nurse moving behind us in the glass.

We didn't stay long. There's an unwritten etiquette to these rooms. You don't overdo the smiles. You don't promise what you can't deliver. You don't stay until you make it about you.

Merk drove me to my house through a dusky, watery light. On the radio, Peter and Gordon sang with gentle, plaintive harmonies: "I don't care what they say, I won't stay in a world without love." Tonight the chorus sounded like a diagnosis. Merk and I didn't speak much. I lay my head on the inside of a rain-soaked window, eyes vacant, feeling like my body wasn't there. My reflection looked older by a decade. Tires hissed on wet streets, stoplights blurred.

At my place, Merk pulled into the driveway and let the engine idle. He looked like he wanted to tell me something. Something that might comfort both of us. But he didn't. He barely looked at me when I climbed out. I shut the door gently, afraid that a harder slam would set off alarms somewhere. I waved, and he lifted two fingers off the wheel, not unkindly, nodded, and drifted back into the dark.

Inside, the world reasserted a poignant normalcy, like a television left on so you wouldn't feel so alone, even though we always are. The smell of spaghetti sauce

Mom was cooking hit me first. Carmel had the rabbit ears in a death grip, tilting them to tune the TV from snow to Channel Eight's Big Time Wrestling. On the screen, Bruno Sammartino sailed from the turnbuckle like some cathedral gargoyle and landed full-chest on a man whose job it was to be crushed. The announcer babbled about "solid punishment" and other annoying superlatives.

"Hey! Why you watchin' that stupid crap? None of it's real, y'know." The words came out before I could put a hand over my mouth.

Carmel didn't blink. "Yeah? Well, it's as real as radio!"

"Shut up!"

"You shut up! At least I know it's all fake. And no one gets hurt, neither."

Her last words bit hard, and I felt a little bubble inside my chest pop.

I climbed the stairs like I was walking up a station's tower ladder in a crosswind. My room was what it always was: a cheap old desk with its worn edges polished by my forearms, shelves where plastic airplane models had replaced books. On the desk, my little gyroscope waited, its string coiled, patiently.

I sat on my bed and pulled the string—zip—and set the spinning top on the tip of my finger. It balanced there, humming in place. The motion hypnotized and calmed me, offering an illusion: that a thing in motion could stay in motion, untouched by drag or gravity.

Mom came in with an armful of clothes that smelled of laundry soap and outside air. A drawer squeaked and accepted a few undershirts and tighty-whities. She noticed me, sitting there still mesmerized by the gyro.

"You okay, sweetie?" she asked, not fussing, just taking attendance.

I watched the orb spin, its silver rim a blur.

"Ma? You ever think about radio?"

She made a little sarcastic sound that meant, "Right. As if…!" Then said, "Oh, 'bout as much as I think about these socks, honey."

"Huh?" I said, genuinely confused, because to me, radio was the water I swam in.

"I mean, it's like, turn on the radio, and sound comes out like… tap water. What's to think?"

"But, what about all the people that make the sound come out?" I pressed, as if by asking, I could keep a certain man in a certain chair behind a certain pane of soundproof glass.

"Oh, I don't worry 'bout that stuff, Tommy. Well, not as much as you."

"How's come?"

"Well, cuz I'm… cleanin' and cooking," she said, closing a drawer with her hip, "and havin' a life. Ooo, why? Did somethin' happen at the station?"

I watched the gyro's spin falter as it developed a little wobble, then uncertainty, and then decay. The tiny axis leaned. The noise of its hum lowered, its pitch turning to a mutter.

"I, I was jus' thinkin' about how nothin' ever… stays the same. Y'know?"

The gyroscope surrendered, fell from my fingertip onto my thigh with a soft thunk. Mom crossed the room and put her hand on my hair, then on the back of my neck.

"Yeah, honey. Nothin' ever does. Dinner's almost ready. Wash up, yeah?"

She left the room inside the happy weather system she always carried, and I sat a moment longer to once more consider the dead gyro cooling in my lap. Downstairs, the TV crowd roared for a "wrassling pin" that was as phony as it looked. Upstairs, I imagined a white room where a woman bounced a ball and a man I admired sooo much looked at the trees in silence.

Fairhill Hospital—cheerful, bright, "open"—had given me a new terror. I wondered if Dicky had seen the Manikin again after we left. Wondered if it stood behind his shoulder like a censor, if the lightning that shot through his brain had made it retreat or just sharpened the Thing's edges. I pictured Dicky's face by the window, the glass turning the outside world into a movie he didn't have to star in anymore. If you're a boy, you think heroes are men who never flinch and just power into unknown dangers, guns blazing. If you're lucky enough to live a little, you learn that real heroes are the only men who do flinch, but walk in anyway.

On my desk, under my elbow, lay a dog-eared card from a station giveaway—a KYW logo in winter blue. I traced the letters with my thumb, the K like arms akimbo, the Y like a wishbone. I wondered if radio could survive dead air, if a heart could be revived by a song, if a mind could be changed by a zap of electricity. Somewhere in the city, a light on a transmitter tower winked through fog to warn planes away. Somewhere else, in a white room that had decided its own mercy, a man slept beneath a blanket. And I wondered if he still knew his name.

I went to the bathroom and ran water over my hands until the hot water made me gasp. The mirror showed a boy whose eyes were older. I drew a circle in the mirror fog and marked a face that had two dots for the nose... and a straight line for the mouth. The world was always trying to make you choose between laughing and crying, but sometimes the only rebellion is to swipe it all away. So I did.

At dinner, Dad asked the usual questions with the usual reluctance, and Mom answered with the usual cheer. Carmel kept her wrestling to herself and her butt in her seat. I chewed and nodded quietly, not completely in the moment.

That night, I dreamed of studio clocks with no hands, of a rubber ball bouncing in an endless corridor, and of a switch flipped, allowing actual electricity into a human brain.

I woke before dawn and lay there in the heavy quiet, waiting for the first small sound of morning: our forced-air furnace clearing its throat. When it came, I let myself breathe again, and I thought, against the better evidence, that air is air, even when it's dead. The trick might be to keep listening until someone speaks into it.

Nine — The Comeback

"One must imagine Sisyphus happy."—Albert Camus

Friday brought Dicky's "procedure." Saturday brought its sad acceptance. Sunday brought forgotten homework and the last spoonful of Mom's sweet gravy scraped from the pan.

But Monday was special. It was Dicky's resurrection!

He'd been gone—hidden away behind Fairhill's white walls, where nobody spoke above a whisper and doors opened onto rooms you didn't want to imagine. Now he was back, pale as copy paper, tie half-knotted, trumpet dangling against his leg like a dead goose.

Merk had been chewing the same cigarette all evening, unlit, teeth grinding paper and tobacco. He'd said little to me before the big show, but the silence was worse than a lecture. His eyes kept flicking down the corridor, where he expected Dicky to bolt before airtime.

"You, uh, you nervous, kid?" Merk finally asked, just before the clock clicked to six-thirty.

I shrugged, trying for nonchalance, but my stomach was a clenched fist. "Lil' bit."

"Yeah, well, me too." He spat tobacco flecks into his palm and tucked the dead butt back in his shirt pocket. "But let's don't be. It's not on me or you. Tonight's all about him."

I entered the familiar Ansaphone booth to get my act together, check the phones, and write down about twenty names Dicky could use to open his homecoming show.

Through the glass of the control room, I could see Chick stacking carts, fingers dancing over switches like a card shark about to fleece the room. The ON AIR sign above the studio door, dark for now, would soon be ready to burn red.

I took off for Dicky's air studio, dropped the pile of fresh names, requests, and dedications on his console, then high-tailed it to a corner vending machine to grab a Clark Bar. There was a cigarette machine next to it, too. But I always chose chocolate over eternal damnation.

As I stood there, peeling the wrapper, Dicky and Merk walked down the hallway together, looking serious, chatting. Merk muttered something I didn't catch, but Dicky nodded. Then he spotted me in the corridor. "Hold up, pal," he called to me. His eyes were tired but softer than I'd seen in weeks.

"Hey, bud! C'mere," he said.

I blinked. "Me?" He nodded slowly and waved me over. I walked up, as sincerely as I could muster, and chirped, "So... um, Dicky... how you feelin'?"

"Meh, good. Thanks. Well, better. Hey, listen, man... uh, about the other day. Merk said I was a real asshole to you."

"Nah. Really? When?" I feigned.

"Yeah. Yeah, I was." He rubbed the back of his neck. "That time when I yelled. I... I... wasn't... myself, see?" He shook his head, ashamed and angry at the same time.

"Aww... 'at's okay. I shouldn't 'a bothered you."

"No, no, no. It was me. I was in a... bad place, y'know? So, I'm really very... sorry." Then Dicky extends his hand for a shake. I was quick to take it and looked down at our grasp, absolutely astounded. Dicky

Peppers was apologizing… to me!? All I could do was nod my head and wish I still had Alvy to share this with.

"It wasn't fair, man. I shouldn't have… Yeah… So… well, uh, thanks."

I shrugged, trying to play it cool, though my ears still burned at the memory. "Aw, it's really okay."

"No. It really isn't." He tilted his head, studying me as if hunting for the right distraction. "Hey, c'mon, walk with me." We entered the soon-to-be-on-air studio like two colleagues. It was the best feeling I'd ever had.

Dicky sat at his console, shuffling ad copy, checking the time, and looking over requests.

"Say, do you remember who won the World Series in 'sixty-two?"

I hesitated, then shrugged.

"Me neither," Dicky said with a wry grin. "Biggest game in the country, front page news, and we can't remember. Ain't that a kick in the head? And that goes for everything—movie stars, presidents, big events. All gone, forgotten… just like that." He snapped his fingers.

"Yeah," I said, fumbling for optimism. "But not everything. I mean, tonight you'll go down in history, Dicky!"

He barked a short laugh, more bitter than amused. "No thanks. Rememberin's for suckers, pal."

"But—you will be," I insisted. "Cuz... you're back on the air!"

He leaned down, hands gripping my shoulders, eyes pinning me in place. "Stick your fingers in a bucket'a water for fifteen years. Then pull it out, and see what impression your hand left."

I stared at him, words caught in my throat.

He stared at the wall. "It's all... pointless, Tommy" he whispered. The words weren't cruel; they were heavy, words I could feel.

I, of course, didn't know what to say. At twelve, you think the world is made of solid things—heroes, World Series, voices on the radio. Hearing him call it pointless was like watching someone drain the color from the sky. Later, I'd puzzle over it in bed. At the time, the only thought I could manage was: Maybe the bucket just needed thicker water. What? C'mon, I was twelve!

Just then, Merk appeared at the door, moving in and clapping his hand against Dicky's back with more force than comfort. "Alright, boys," he said, grinning like a stage manager pushing reluctant actors onto the stage. "Time to get this freakin' circus rolling. You, out! Go man the damn phones, and you..." I sped off to Ansaphone-land, but heard Merk lean closer to Dicky, his voice dropping. "If you don't feel it tonight, don't be a hero. We'll call this off. The whole damn thing. Nothin' says you gotta do this. We pull the plug, and I take all the heat. Got that?"

Merk's words thudded in my chest. Pull the plug on Dicky Peppers? The man who'd taught half of Cleveland what a joke sounded like on the radio? It felt like saying you'd snuff out a lighthouse because the bulb flickered. Anyway, I got set among the phones and requests with my heart knocking in my ears.

Inside the KYW news booth, as the hour neared seven o'clock, Jon Scott Trotter practiced his foot pedal tap: dit-dit-dit-dit-dit-dit, the drumbeat of urgency. He glanced at his script, cleared his throat, and waited for his cue.

"And that's K-W- Double News banner lines. Next report at any moment! I'm Jon Scott Trotter," he said, voice crisp, "Standing by for the World's Greatest Trumpet Player—on the Swingin' Dicky Peppers Show!"

Chick jammed a cart into place.

The second hand slid to the top with the seven p.m. "Beep!"

The cue light snapped on.

Inside the booth, Dicky lifted the trumpet. His fingers shook, but the horn caught the light. He pressed the mouthpiece to his lips and blew a honk sharp enough to cut glass.

In an instant, the sound of showtime was everywhere.

"Here… is love in your ear!" the Jingle Singers crooned, exciting as ever.

The trumpet blast followed—louder, wilder, defiant.

"Hubba-hubba!" the Sonovox snarled.

"With K-Y-W's Swingin' Dicky Peppers!" shouted the singers.

And just like that, Merk let out a breath he'd been holding for a day and a half.

Dicky didn't just start the show—he attacked it. If you were listening on the other end of a kitchen radio, you'd swear he'd spent the week at a spa, not in a white room where clocks didn't matter. But inside the booth, we saw it: the forced grin, the ashen cheeks, the perspiration already beading.

"STUNNER!" he roared, chest out, elbows cocked as if he was conducting the air itself. "It's your Guru of Horniness, more powerful than fifty thousand blow dryers combined!"

His patter flew like a lit fuse—names, places, a city mapped out in shout-outs. "Hi to Peppers People all over mid-America... Sharon and Blake in Cleveland Heights, Cass and Mindy in Mansfield. Hi and good luck at State to the Purple and Gold Rangers of Lakewood High's wrestling team. Ooo, hubba-hubba. Sweaty men!"

On cue, the tape—our famous "sexy woman" drop-in—purred back: a velvet "Ohhhh! Mmmm." Somewhere in town, a boy punched his best friend on the arm and said, "I wanna make a girl sound like that!"

From my post behind the Ansaphone glass, I could feel Merk's eyes on me: See? He's flyin', he winked. But I also saw the tremor in Dicky's left hand—just a whisper, the kind you notice only when you've studied every detail of Dicky Peppers. Chick kept the music flowing, the level meters peaking, and the board a field of tiny suns under his fingers.

We had him aloft. But how long could he stay there?

Hour one of the show passed, and Dicky was sensational, better than ever. Still, it made me think whoever said, "the show must go on," must have been the guy who owned the theater. Because, did it? I mean, really? Anyway, it was KYW news time again, and I sensed this was my chance.

Down the corridor, Jon Scott Trotter laid into the mic. Then tapped that pedal under his desk like a woodpecker—dit-dit-dit-dit-dit-dit—the rhythm that screamed, "News is happening, pay attention, ya dumb jamokes!" He loosened his tie and took a breath.

"The Beatles Banned in Boom Town!" he announced, relishing the capital Bs like a man savoring prime rib. "Mayor Ralph Locher says no more shaggy-haired mop-tops allowed in ANY Cleveland city-owned facility!"

If I'd been older, I might've snorted at the politics of it. At twelve, it knocked me sideways. The Beatles… banned? Even I knew that was bullshit! It was like telling Lake Erie to take a week off from being a lake.

As Trotter chewed the scenery with "news," I pushed open the deejay booth studio door during the pee break.

The room met me the way a church meets you when you sneak in. I had crossed into the Holy of Holies, I thought. The Sanctum Sanctorum. It was just me. First time I'd dared to be in there alone.

The "air chair"—Dicky's chair—wore the shape of his restlessness. The brass of the trumpet winked at me from the desk, an invitation and a dare. I touched the arm of the chair the way you touch a relic when you're not sure your hands are clean. Then I let my fingertips slide to the horn. It was heavier than I'd expected. I caught my own face in the bell—funhouse-mirror warped, googly-eyed, and ridiculous.

"Woah," I breathed. "Fab gear!"

Outside the studio door, in its round window, Merk passed by, glanced in, saw me with the trumpet, and actually smiled. He shook his head in a "you rascal, you" kind of way and beckoned Dicky from the hall. They peered like schoolkids daring each other to look.

So, the booth and I were alone. I raised the horn, blew a honk that skittered around the room, then leaned toward the mic and let my best "puke announcer" radio voice fly.

"Hiya-hiya kids! It's the Tommy Bee Show! With musical honey that's right on the money!"

I pointed across to the empty studio control room as if Chick was waiting for the cue and did my best live version of the station's most notorious "sexy woman" drop-in. I deepened my voice into the slink:

"Ohhhh, Mmmm! All right, let's see who's buzzin' 'round the ol' Tommy Bee-hive tonight!"

From the stack of slips on Dicky's desk, I plucked a name like a prize from a fishbowl.

"My pollinator's pointed at the Panthers of Euclid High. Hello to Queen Vicky-Lynn and her drone, Morgan!"

I jabbed a finger toward the imaginary sound effects and crooned into the next one.

"Hubba-hubba! Hey to Sam, and Patty, Lloyd and Marlene… Ooo, be careful of Lloyd's stinger-dinger, there, Marlene."

I blew another honk.

"Hi to worker-bees Sally, Mike…"

Then the door pushed open.

I turned, horn half-raised.

Dicky stood in the frame with a paperback dangling from two fingers. Merk hovered behind him, arms folded, a grin chewing at the corner of his mouth. For an instant, raw fear hit me and then melted through the floor—because Dicky's face wasn't furious. It was amused, tired, and a little surprised that something could still surprise him.

"...Oh, shit!" I blurted, scrambling up for the chair, the trumpet clanking as I set it down. "Gosh. I'm sorry, Dicky. I was jus'—"

He raised a palm, generous. "S'okay, kiddo."

He eased into the air throne with the relief of a pilot returning to his natural altitude.

"You, ah, you actually did good."

I blinked. "Did I?!"

"Yeh. Nice patter."

"Wow. Thanks, Dicky! That means... everything to me. Aw, I—I wish I could be a deejay. Someday I'm gonna be just like you."

He made a soft phfft, almost affectionate, almost pitying. "What? And live the Carney life!? No, no. No offense, but, uh, I wouldn't wish for that."

"Why not? Everyone knows you... and loves you!"

That did it—something flashed across his eyes like a storm crossing. "Everyone, huh? You ever think how many people there are in the world, kid?"

I swallowed. "A lot?"

"And most don't know, don't listen, and don't care."

I quieted, the bravado evaporating. "I... I care."

For a heartbeat, the room steadied. He looked through me, not at me, like he was remembering his own 12-year-old self. Then he held out a paperback, the corners bent, the spine softened by half a life in pockets: *The Myth of Sisyphus*, by Albert Camus.

"Here. Read that. Let me know what you think."

The cover stared up at me, severe as a math teacher. I squinted at the name. "C, CAM-us?"

He corrected me gently, almost playfully. "Ca-MOO. Like a cow. French guy. Tells a story 'bout a fella who's gotta roll a boulder up a mountain, and when he gets to the top, it just rolls back down, so he's gotta start over."

I made a face. "Why?"

He snapped his fingers. "Exactly! And he does it for eternity."

I hugged the book to my chest like a shield. "No thanks. I'd sooner be a radio star!"

His smile thinned to paper. "I wish you knew what it's like to be successful at something that doesn't matter."

I flinched. "But—but, NO! It does matter…"

From the monitor, Chick's voice swam back in, flattened and practical: "Comin' back in thirty, Pep."

Dicky dipped toward me, his breath warm with mints. "Look, buddy. Do… do somethin' meaningful with, uh, your… rock, okay? Promise me. Do that, huh?"

I nodded because no other answer existed. Sitting in the Ansaphone studio, Merk checked the clock and tapped the window. "COME ON! LET'S GO!

I ran to the door with the paperback crimping my fingers, eased it open just enough to slip through, and tugged it shut.

The hallway stretched long and bright, a fluorescent river. I walked without quite knowing where my feet intended to go, flipping open the book to a random page I couldn't possibly digest. Words like boulders: "absurd," "revolt," "freedom." I felt too young for all three, and yet—they were the only big ideas on offer tonight.

Behind me, through the glass, Dicky was back—voice hot, trumpet bright, the city pulling his music through its vents.

At the corner where the corridor bent toward the Ansaphones, a shadow separated itself from the wall. No, it was Merk. Don't get ahead of me! He'd been waiting, which is to say, he knew boys; he knew that sometimes we need someone to materialize when we feel we're most invisible.

"You all right, Tommy-boy?" he asked, keeping his voice low. The red ON AIR sign above the door to Dicky's studio demanded reverence, even from the hallway.

I nodded, swallowed, and nodded again. "He gave me a book."

Merk's mouth twitched. "He would." He jerked his chin toward the cover. "You gonna read it?"

"I dunno. It, it looks hard." I thumbed a page as if I was checking the grain on a piece of wood. "He said it's about a guy who pushes a rock forever."

Merk's eyes did a slow roll up to the ceiling and back. "Yeah, that makes sense." He let the silence sit for a second, then hooked a thumb toward the booth. "Listen. He's fine in there now, but if things get too hot—if he staggers—you'll see me move. What do you do?" He tipped his head, wanting a promise.

"Um, stay out of the way," I said.

"That's my boy." He scrubbed a hand over the back of his neck. For a tough guy, he carried so much tenderness you could trip over it. "Kid... whatever he told you, he... he meant it, y'know." He shifted, uncomfortable with sentiment. "Anyway. Let's spot him. If he wobbles, we catch."

We stepped back inside Ansaphone-ville and watched Dicky from the glass, like two moths to a single lamp. Inside, Dicky was soaring again! He faked a trumpet riff and slid into a jingle that fit like a snap-on tie. A pro's pro.

Some time passed, and I headed to the restroom for a quick squirt, but halfway down, I almost collided with Dicky himself.

He'd stepped out to the hallway between another "twin spin"—alone—like a diver coming up fast to see the sky. The sweat line at his hair had thickened; he'd stripped off his jacket; his shirt clung to him like a loyal pet. When he saw me, he stopped. So did I.

"Oh, Tommy, one more thing." Dicky's eyes softened, then sharpened, then softened again. "I mean—if I ever made you think this…"—he gestured vaguely at the booth—"is what a life has to be…" he shook his head. "That's not what I meant, okay? I mean, if it's your thing, fine. I mean, we're all different, right? Just don't let it become… everything."

It took me a second to understand what was happening. This was not about catching me in his chair. It felt like a warning. About being careful about wanting something that might eat me alive, especially if I hadn't thought things through all the way.

"But I want this," I said, barely above a whisper. "I love it."

He gave a little smile that was mostly grief wearing joy's coat. "Yeah. I remember that feelin'." He reached out, squeezed the paperback still in my hand.

"Just… read the book, hm? And… try to… really help people, okay?" He turned and vanished back to his studio.

I didn't know it then, but that would be the final thing he'd ever say to me.

The ON AIR sign blinked back to life. Merk came up behind me.

"He's burnin' the candle at both ends," he muttered. "And I'm a'scared they ain't no wax left."

I didn't answer. I was twelve. All I knew was that Dicky Peppers was back on the air, sounding larger than life, and somehow that meant Cleveland was safe for another night.

By nine o'clock, the booth smelled like sweat, smoke, and burnt coffee. Dicky was still flying, but the lines under his eyes deepened, his skin more pale. He punched his patter out with manic glee, horn blasts between songs like exclamation points carved in steel.

Chick grinned despite himself. Merk didn't.

I pressed closer to the glass, watching Dicky's chest heave between jokes. His lips twitched around words, forcing cheer into every syllable. The longer he talked, the clearer it became: this wasn't a comeback, it was a battle.

He leaned into the trumpet again, blasting out a riff that nearly cracked the levels. When the record spun and the mic went cold, he slumped in the chair, wiping his forehead with a crumpled handkerchief. For a second, his face looked naked, raw, stripped of all the showman's armor. Then the cue light flared, and he was back, smiling like nothing in the world had ever hurt.

Merk muttered, "Jesus, Pep. He's gonna kill himself on the air. And for what?"

By the time the show edged toward closing, the tension was tight as piano wire. Tommy Bee—the little fantasy I'd played—lightened my chest a bit, but the Camus book weighed heavily. Dicky had handed me something I didn't know how to hold.

At the final break, Chick's voice crackled through the monitor: "Comin' back in thirty, Pep."

Dicky nodded, sweat running down his temples. Then I saw it. That vacant fear again, the flash in his eyes, one I'd seen before. It was quick and passing, but it was there. Dicky stared numbly at the wall—at nothing.

Shit. Was it back? Did the Faceless Thing that once invaded his psyche return to nest? Maybe it was just exhaustion, but Dicky sure looked like he was about to crack. He bent toward the mic, hands gripping the desk like a man bracing against a wave. Could he get through this?

Sure, he could! And did! When the light snapped red. Dicky sounded charged up, playing the part of Cleveland's wacky Guru of Horniness, still the funniest voice blasting out across Ohio, his horn honking in victory.

But seeing that small crack, the only hiccup he had allowed all show, haunted me and made me sad. Maybe it was possible for a sick deejay to sound great in twenty-second bursts, but he wasn't better yet. I could tell.

I slipped into the hallway, relieved it was over, thoughts rolling around in my head like pebbles I couldn't yet stack. Merk followed a few paces behind, silent, his eyes fixed on the air booth.

We didn't know—not yet—but this would be the last night for Dicky Peppers on KYW. What none of us knew was what waited in the gray light of the next morning.

Ten — Pulling the Plug

The play was a great success, but the audience was a disaster." —Oscar Wilde

KYW's general manager, Art Bocello, kept his office and his heart cold enough to freeze milk. The morning light came in from behind him, through Venetian blinds in thin, dark stripes that made everything look as if a government page had been redacted. Art had a reel-to-reel machine perched on a side credenza—a proud, leather-wrapped beast that ate recording tape like licorice. On the wall hung a crooked certificate from some sales convention in Cincinnati, last year's National Association of Broadcasters calendar not yet removed, and a framed letter from a grocery chain praising his "synergy," which meant "Thanks for not screwing up our ad buy."

He fiddled with the waist of his light-blue Sansabelt pants, puffed on a smoke, then leaned over the tape deck and hit PLAY. The hubs spun, and Art listened like a hanging judge.

Out of the speaker oozed the kind of optimism you can only buy in sixty-second ad blocks. It was the Krakus Polish ham commercial again.

"Great in a sandwich or as a Sunday main dish, you just can't beat it..." The recorded commercial announcer gushed.

Ken sat across from the desk, the chair two inches lower than Art's by design. His hands were folded in a way that said, "I'm listening," while his eyes said, "I'm calculating." He wore a permanent frown.

Then came the curveball. Dicky's voiceover and, in between the recording, the unmistakable sideways pitch of a man who couldn't leave a radio ad alone even if it was paying his salary. Dicky interacted within the pauses left by the recorded announcer, injecting his own mocking, sarcastic, and hilarious satire. It not only lampooned the sponsor's message, it was a social commentary on the stupid drone of most radio advertising, which I thought actually made the repetitive and stale commercial more memorable.

"Well, not at the table," Dicky interjected.

Art's jaw stopped chewing. He froze in a posture of rage that hadn't yet decided which direction to explode. The tape rolled on.

"So, get crackin' with delicious Krakus Polish hams today!" concluded the ad man's voice.

Dicky paused and chuckled before reading the live end tag."Um…I'll tell ya this much. With a name like Krakus, it's gotta be Polish."

From Chick's cartridge bay came Dicky's novelty snarl that had become part of the show's furniture: the Sonovox, leering and cartoon-sincere all at once—"Hubba-hubba!"

Art exploded.

"JESUS FUCK!"

He stabbed the STOP button so hard that the reel-to-reel machine almost fell on the floor. Art fumed. You could almost see the steam rising from his ass. Then he mashed PLAY again, as if evidence needed to hear itself twice to be admissible. The tape dove back in mid-sin.

"Krakus Ham," Dicky said, "for all your slapping pleasure." Then immediately corrected the dick joke: "SHOPPING..."

The "sexy woman" drop-in cooed, "Ohhhhh, mmm," as if she'd been diddled.

Art smacked the switch off again, the desk receiving his fist like an anvil. The phone trembled in its cradle. Paperweights shifted allegiance. He glared at the machine.

"CHRIST!" He barked, a vein in his temple pulsing blue.

As if to prove he wasn't hearing things, Art reversed the tape and listened again to make sure. Dicky's line wowed up one more time, like a kid sticking his tongue out from behind his mother's skirt.

Click. Silence. Art's eyes bulged, and his cigarette ash grew an inch longer.

He pointed a finger at Ken like a pistol. "I want that filthy, smug sonofabitch off my air NOW! No one fucks with my commercials, Ken! NOBODY! It's goddamn insubordination! If I was still fighting at Anzio, that prick would be shot!"

A folder of affidavits slid under Art's palm, and he flung it across the desk. Papers fanned out in a white squall of numbers.

"Look! Look'a that! That's over four grand in revenue! GONE! Shit! Meldrum and Fewsmith want his head. Kroger's threatenin' to sue! I gotta do ten-to-one make-goods just to keep these fuckers happy! AND they say they're gonna bring in lawyers, Ken, lawyers, to check our skimmers lookin' for more 'contract violations!' FUCK ME..." he tugged at his face, "with a goddamn traffic cone."

Ken lifted both hands, palms visible, a man showing he carried no weapon besides a Rolodex. "Hey, it, it's one mistake, one time. Most people didn't even hear it."

Art's laugh had no humor. "Yeah, well, the people that count, DID! I want the bastard gone!"

Ken tried the only lever that sometimes moved men like Art: math. "Art, at night, Dick's got huge T-S-Ls. A seventy-one percent share... his A-Q-H's are off the..."

"I said FIRE HIS ASS, NOW! Just stick another one of your fuckin' monkeys in there to tell goddamn jokes, KEN! What's the problem!? Christ Almighty!"

Ken closed his mouth and opened his briefcase. Even a clever man knows which tides he can't swim against. He gathered the scattered paperwork into a shape that suggested order, because order is the only lie that makes sense at a radio station in panic.

On the tape machine, the reels sat poised, the tape drooping like crepe paper. Dicky's joke—too funny to leave off-air, too expensive to leave on—still echoed in the room.

The live copy tag clearly read, "Shopping pleasure." Dicky found the juvenile slipstream and, because he was Dicky, slid in. There are words the public can forgive and words the sponsors cannot. "Slapping" is only funny until a lawyer writes it down.

Ken stood. "Okay. I'll… handle it," he said.

Art adjusted his Sansabelt again.

I wasn't in the room. I was allergic to offices, but word travels down hallways the way smoke finds vents. By the time the story reached me, Art had chewed his cigarette filter down to its wool, and Ken had left the office so fast that his tie flew over his shoulder.

Yep. That's what did it. Dicky got canned by a canned ham.

That's how I told it to myself later, alone in my room, holding the Camus book and wondering if Sisyphus ever took a day off. A radio personality had forgotten he was also the voice of a corporation. It was guilt by association. The ad buy won. It always would.

Ken's office looked like a comparative photo study titled "Before Pictures." He had a talent for chaos camouflaged as readiness: stacks of rate cards, music surveys, and ashtrays around his desk that reminded me of archipelagos. On a shelf, plaques so vague they could congratulate any five-year-old after a Tee-ball game—"Outstanding Achievement," "Excellence,"

"Leadership"—which in radio only meant, "Congrats! You survived another year!"

Dicky came in quietly, which wasn't his way. He closed the door behind him without flair, took a seat, and waited. The last time he'd been in there, he'd perched on the chair's edge, bouncing his knee, "apologizing" for his successful "Louie, Louie" stunt. Today, he sat back, and the seat claimed him.

Ken nervously cleared a rectangle on his desk by moving a mountain of papers two inches to the left. He tried on a smile and found it didn't fit. He looked down at a severance check in a white envelope, then at Dicky.

"So, ah, Dick. Listen. We, um, we've decided to go in a… different direction at night, see? So, uh, thanks for your, uh, your help and, y'know, good luck."

Ken slid the check across his desk unceremoniously, as if offering a coaster for a drink. Then extended his hand, like they were closing a small business loan. Dicky looked at the hand, then at Ken's face, then at the check. Dicky didn't shake. He let the uncomfortable moment stretch and didn't whine or argue. Why get dramatic now? Shit, he'd been "let go" before at other stations. The decision came from the top, and Dicky knew he held losing cards. He just plucked up the money—like a man pulling off a Band-Aid—stood, tucked the check into the inner pocket of his jacket, and left. No, goodbye, not even a fuck you.

Ken's face held in "pleasantly nonplussed" mode for one, two, three seconds, then sagged back into "man who needs a smoke." He looked around for his cigarettes and found one of the five packs he'd started staring back.

Ol' Ken, there, was eventually caught and slapped on the wrist for cheating—for telling his deejays to give the wrong time to influence Arbitron ratings.

That's a sentence I still carry around like a smooth stone, rubbing it sometimes just to feel its shape. It makes a man sound wicked in a way the public understands, but in radio, it's just an old trick from the bottom of a drawer. Make midnight come two minutes later, steal morning drive from a competitor by counting "8:58" a little longer than the clock would prefer, pretend commercials are fewer by moving the minutes around like you're peeling cards from the top and the bottom at the same time. If you never learned to lie to a clock, you never really worked in radio.

And for this—something that Art called, "Damn good work!"— Ken Apati eventually became the top dog at Pegasus Satellite Radio and made a fortune programming giant jukeboxes from the sky… without any personality jocks to deal with. The future didn't need Dicky's trumpet or anybody's heartbeat; it needed a playlist that never called in sick. One hundred fifty channels of music and talk that never got sued by a meat company.

Ken finally located a pack of Viceroys under a folder labeled "Remotes," tapped a cigarette loose, and struck a match. Smoke made a gray halo around his face. I thought a rope around his neck would be more apropos.

He picked up the phone and dialed without looking—muscle memory from a thousand questionable favors. When a voice answered, Ken tilted his chair, put his feet up on a stack of proposals, and went to work.

"Ronnie… get me Bill Barrett at *The Cleveland Press.*"

Of course, he would. Radio doesn't end on the air, it ends in myth. If you can't sell a story to the local paper, the paper will sell one about you, and you can't control its content.

Here's what wasn't in any KYW "confidential memo." In the great ledger of sins, Dicky's joke outweighed the years he helped grow the station's audience. I know that sounds melodramatic. It's also math, money, and a business-perfected PR technique called "covering your ass."

Ken's pitch to the newspaper would read more smoothly. It would mention "creative differences," and "format consistency," and "ongoing commitment to our advertisers." It might even "regret to inform." It would not say that a man had stopped in a hallway and apologized to a kid for teaching him to want a thing that might chew him up.

Dicky never told me the news himself. Word ricocheted around—copy desk to newsroom to switchboard to a bench I occupied in the hallway. The way I heard it, someone said, "they clipped Pep," like a boxer's corner man telling the fighter the cut's too deep and "the commission" won't let him go the next round. I carried the news down the corridor in my chest and didn't drop it until I was home, in bed, staring at the ceiling, listening to KYW that I still couldn't turn off.

You want me to say I was angry at Art? I was, sure. But I was also twelve and secretly impressed that a man could work himself into such a lather over a ham commercial. You want me to say I hated Ken? I didn't. He did the job the station asked him to do, which is harder to forgive than malice. Malice at least has personality.

But, I get it. It was about station revenue, commerce, and money. Without that sweet green, there wouldn't be a KYW. It was also a chilling example of how self-censorship stops memorable, mind-stretching satire from happening in the moment. Most disturbingly, Dicky's firing was left as an example for all other air personalities to "watch your mouth" and pick your battles. This was business. And business rules.

They say radio is ephemeral, that it vanishes as it's made. That it's "disposable media," all glue and glitter that creates an entire universe, and then it's gone. And that's exactly how it grew to be designed. But there are consequences in such a design. What may not have been considered is that Radioland, in my case, also built an unintended fantasy in a sensitive young boy's mind. It's what architects and evolutionary biologists call a spandrel—a thing seen as a useless byproduct, a leftover space that sort of just happens in architecture, biology, and even in the natural processes of business. And within that spandrel, my mind was flooded with delight, possibilities, and heartbreak.

Anyone who'd ever curled up in a dark bed tent at night with the transistor speaker turned low so as not to wake a house knows it. The voice in there is real. The company is real. The jokes are wedges that pry open your eyes and let you see things as senseless and absurd as they are. And in Radioland, that's dangerous. Any critical thinking is. Dicky had been that voice—the rascal uncle who made me laugh, the trumpet blast that made me feel less alone. Watching him get measured by a sponsor's ruler hurt like an infected paper cut.

Art told himself he was protecting the business. In a way, he was. A disk jockey isn't religion; he's a line item. Art's Sansabelt pants chafed at the waist because numbers tighten decisions better than feelings. Besides, he had a mortgage and maybe a head cold; he didn't have time for a person who could ruin a buy with a punchline. The sixties for me was a drawer full of such spandrels, and a man in a French-cuffed dress shirt with flashy cufflinks would do anything to keep his afloat.

Ken, on the other hand, loved the game more than the players. The players get old, but the game just gets better. He'd learned that if you kept the tunes spinning, no one would notice when you switched out the players. I don't even mean that as an insult. Ken was simply built to survive.

As for Dicky, I can't tell you exactly what he did in the hours after the severance check. Maybe he went to Otto Moser's bar and stared at a beer until it told him a new story. Maybe he drove to the lake and sat till the seagulls decided he wasn't going to feed them. The thing about radio is you can't save it up. When the light goes from RED to DARK, you have whatever you've put into the people who listened. That's your bank account.

I know what I did. I carried *The Myth of Sisyphus* around like a brick. I read the same paragraph six times and pretended I understood it on the seventh, which is what most adults do anyway. Camus said a man forever pushing a rock could be happy if he decided that pointlessness was the point. It's the paradox and absurdity of life: everything is important, and nothing is. I sensed that was the essential idea that Dicky could never fully negotiate. Maybe the joke about Krakus hams was a tiny act of rebellion against his corporate overlords, the last good riff in a long solo.

Art would tell the sales team they were lucky to cut their losses. Ken would tell his wife at dinner that night that he'd had to do something "unpleasant but necessary," and then he slept like a baby. The sponsor would tell their agency to triple-check the next batch of copy and underline any phrases that could be twisted by the clown prince of deejays. And the city would turn its dial at seven the next night and find a new, cheerful voice telling them not to worry, that the music was still there, and that the world is the same as yesterday.

Well, it wasn't.

I could tell the station wasn't the same. I could hear it in the way Chick hit a jingle a beat early, in the way Trotter tapped his foot pedal harder than it deserved. You don't need a statue to prove a man like Dicky existed; sometimes all you need are the dents he left in your mind.

"Ronnie... get me Bill Barrett at *The Cleveland Press*." Ken had a one-sided story to tell the paper about format changes and exciting new directions. He would not mention Krakus by name. He would not mention "slapping pleasures." He would say "parted ways" and "mutual decision." He would send a headshot of Dicky that didn't look like Dicky and get a quote signed with a "radio name" that Dicky hadn't chosen.

If you're waiting for justice, you won't find it in radio. When I peeked in on that sales meeting on my first day, that word never came up. Sure, it's discussed in books—justice, censorship, democracy. Maybe it's better to talk through such ideas on the porch with a friend over a cheap beer. Business won't consider such ephemera; how could it with blinders on, always focused on money? So, it makes up its own rules and lies in the telling. Sometimes, when I'm honest with myself, I think that's all life ever is.

The tape in Art's office would be bulk-erased by that afternoon, a buzzing magnet wiping the evidence so clean that even the oxide couldn't remember. But I do. I remember the commercial's buttery promise, and Dicky slipping the knife in between the words without drawing blood. I imagined Art's face—red and righteous—and Ken—already carefully composing dismissive words to heal a fairly insignificant wound. Mostly, I remember the empty feeling under it all: something that mattered so terribly much to me didn't matter a whit to them, but the world kept spinning anyway.

It was over.

ELEVEN — Aftermath

"All changes, even the most longed for, have their melancholy; for what we leave behind us is a part of ourselves."—Anatole France

The end didn't come with herald trumpets. Not the kind you could hear, anyway. It came with slammed doors and angry words, and GM Art Bocello's office was the epicenter of it all. A place too cold for normal humans, even in late winter, Art kept his AC running. It was a small, refrigerated country ruled by a man with a pen behind his ear and a blood pressure that could pop corn. His carpet had a worn path, evidence of too many hasty decisions.

Later that same morning, after the news of Dicky's firing bounced around, Merk marched into Art's office with the confidence of a man who'd already made peace with unemployment. He stood in the doorway, hands at his sides, mouth curled into an unfriendly smile.

He didn't knock. He didn't need to. If you've ever seen a man decide to quit a whole era, you know the posture: loose shoulders, mouth easy, eyes clear. Merk said it like he was ordering lunch. Not loud. Not snarled. Calmly. The words floated in and landed on Art's desk, right next to his always-glacial coffee. Calm words cut like a knife when a man like Art expects you to beg.

"Never," Merk said, calm as a priest. "Art, I wouldn't go back on street sales for you if you kissed the taint under my balls! Everything you touch turns to shit, man. Why? Cuz, you, you're a goddamn prick, Art."

"Now hold on there, Keag—," Art growled.

Merk interrupted, "Wait, wait. There was something else, too. What was it?"

Art's left eye twitched as he steamed.

"Oh, yeah. I hope you fuckin' drop dead."

Merk didn't wait. He slammed the office door with a finality that shook a paper calendar into a new month.

On the other side, Art detonated! His muffled voice blew through the door cracks like fog from a tea kettle.

"Oh, NO! No, no, NO ya don't! ME? I'M the prick? HUH? NO! You! YOU'RE the prick, Keagels!

You were there to STOP that jagoff! YOU! DON'T you walk out on ME!"

The door whipped open, and there stood Art, his face the exact shade of a stop sign but with bulging neck veins. He pointed at the air as if Merk had left a ghost he could still berate.

"YOU don't get the last laugh here, MERK, ya HEAR!? Fuck YOU! Ya goddamn loser! LOSER!"

Merk didn't flinch. He smirked, half pity, half amusement, then walked away, refusing to give Art the dignity of a reply. You don't argue with a man who's busy drowning, you let him splash. Some victories may be silent, but their impact can be heard for miles.

I wish I could tell you that Art's head exploded and showered the office with canceled receipts. I wish I could tell you he learned something grand. The truth is stranger.

Ol' Art got promoted. Climbed right up the greasy pole to President and CEO of Westinghouse Broadcast. That's the world of Radioland—promotions were like heart attacks. They didn't arrive because you deserved them; they arrived because your number came up. And sure enough, by '73, rumor had it Art's ticker gave out, the veins in his neck finally winning their long war against his chest. Make of that what you will. I suppose the body keeps better score than the boardroom.

After school that day, I took an early bus downtown and met Merk back at Otto Moser's bar, that local watering hole populated by radio, TV, and newspaper people. The table rocked because somebody stole the coaster stuck below to keep it level. The place had the acrid smell of tobacco smoke of all kinds—cigarettes, cigars, pipes—stinks that stick. The paneling, dark, old oak, thick as sermons, carved with names that meant the world to a handful of drunks in 1958.

Moser's was half full of press guys and second-string news directors. Everyone had a story to tell, and most of them ended in someone else's humiliation.

An elderly lady stood, finishing a drink with a tiny umbrella in it. She was some news analyst from

Channel 5 who'd I'd seen on TV, but was too young to find her commentaries watchable. The short woman was all frou-frou—in a long, dead animal coat (mink most likely), overly rouged cheeks on pale skin, and bright red lipstick that "complemented" her curled, thinning auburn-colored hair. She walked up to our table, put a cashmere-gloved hand on Merk's shoulder, glanced at me, and said, "So, Merk. Still corrupting the youth of Cleveland, I see."

Merk chuckled uncomfortably and replied, "Somethin' like that, Dot. Oh, Dorothy, meet Tommy."

Dorothy bowed her head, "Young man." Then to Merk, "So, I hear that you're back on the beach."

"You heard right, Dotty."

Dorothy patted his face and winked. "Mmhm. Keep your head down, dear." And off she walked to her day job.

"Who was that?" I asked.

"Ach. Someone who thinks she's still hot shit because she interviewed Hitler one time," he growled. Then the sad news began. Merk told me everything that happened with Dicky that morning and that he'd quit his job over it. That meant I was out, too, of course. Yeah. I was heartbroken. Radio had actually broken up with me!

I sat across from Merk, tears cutting tracks down my cheeks. Not the one-tear-of-a-brave-boy you see in the movies. Not elegant. Saltwater gushed, and I couldn't stop it.

Merk had a copy of *The Cleveland Press* folded to a headline that might as well have been a punch to the teeth: "KYW Deejay Fired for On-Air Remarks," by Bill Barrett. He held it like a dead bird you're not sure where to bury.

"Bastids. Lyin' sons'abitches!" Merk said,

He slid the paper across to me, abruptly. "Here. Read that! Ga'head."

I wiped my face with the heel of my hand and focused on the black river of type. The words wriggled for a second, the way words do when your eyes are still leaking. Then they settled, and I made my mouth say them.

"Program Director Ken Apati says he was shocked and unaware of the s, s... sexual in... innuendo Pepper's made on his program?" The word "innuendo" felt like a dagger in a dictionary—sharp, wrong, and far too formal for the Dicky I knew.

Merk snatched back the page as if it had tried to bite me. He slammed it flat on the table hard enough to bounce the salt shakers.

"BullSHIT! The fuckin' jagoff knew Dicky's act! Ken'ed pat him on the back for all the shit he done!"

I sobbed harder, the kind of crying that embarrasses while it's happening. Merk's jaw flexed. "Goddamn bastids! So, K-Y comes out smellin' like a rose, and Dicky takes it up the ass. FUCK!"

The bar looked over, then looked away, the way bars do when men loudly drop eff bombs.

I hiccupped more than I breathed, then a hyperventilated sound escaped that I didn't know I could make. Merk's hand went flat on the paper, and for a second, I thought he might tear the news in half, and the story would then be untrue.

Instead, he reached across the table. His hand, rough and surprisingly gentle, "Sorry, Tommy-boy. Stuff like this happens at every station I ever worked for. It's just... radio, kid." He squeezed my fingers, then leaned

262

back with a sigh that sounded like the last air in a balloon. "Oh, which reminds me…"

He reached under the table and pulled up a plain brown grocery bag, oil-stained at the bottom, and crunched tight at the top. He pushed it toward me with a little nod.

"Here. Dicky wanted'cha to have this. G'wan, Tommy. S'for you."

I slid the package closer, hands trembling, and tore the top open. Inside was Dicky's old trumpet—beat-up, dented along the bell, valves sticking like arthritic fingers, its mouthpiece gleaming in bright defiance. But it was his. The brass still smelled faintly of spit, cologne, and the ghost of every riff he'd ever blasted into Cleveland's night sky.

I slid it out and held it like a baby, like a relic, like a grenade, all at once. For a moment, I thought I could hear him honking that ridiculous "hubba-hubba" right beside me.

I wanted to raise it to my lips right there and blow until the windows shook and managers in their

Sansabelt pants ran in and apologized to everybody. Instead, I set it on the table, reverently.

Around us, the bar resumed its pretending. A man laughed a little too hard at a story he'd told before. A waitress balanced three mugs and a life. Behind the counter, the TV ran a silent wrestling match, two men faking violence as an act of kindness for people who needed a place to channel their rage.

"Now what?" I asked, voice small as a radio under a blanket.

Merk leaned back. The light over our table made a halo of his cigarette smoke. He looked like a statue of a saint in a church that had been converted to a pool hall.

"Now?" He shrugged, the softest movement. "Now we keep goin'. Or we don't. That's the trick, kid. No one tells you when to stop loving something. It just... stops letting you in." He must've thought about his own breakups—maybe with women, or other shows at other stations, and with the acceptance that a man could be loyal to a frequency, and the frequency never quite returned the favor.

"Listen," he said, pointing to the trumpet. "That ain't a trophy, okay. It's a reminder, ah, a tool. When you're ready to make a noise wit it, you will. And if you don't? That's okay, too. Not everything you love has to love you back."

I nodded as if I understood. I didn't. Not yet. What I understood was that I wanted to walk out into the afternoon and make the day be about anything else.

You want me to say the city mourned that day? It didn't. It turned the dial and found another cheerful voice. That's one of radio's cruel magic tricks: it replaces itself fast. Another voice said good evening, another jingle kissed the hour, another engineer watched the needles and thought about payday. Somewhere in the suburbs, a kid laughed at a joke I would've laughed at, and the tower light kept blinking its lonely safety code to airplanes that didn't care who had been fired… or quit.

Merk reached for his wallet, found it, and turned a few bills into a quiet exit. He stood, the paper headline abandoned on the table like the skin a snake leaves when it outgrows itself.

On the way to the door, he put one hand on my shoulder and steered me through the dark swing of the bar like a tug guiding a ship that didn't trust the canal. Outside, the light was the kind Cleveland specializes in—gray, pretending to be silver if you squint.

"C'mon, kid," he said. "Let's get some air."

We walked nowhere in particular. That's the best direction after a goodbye.

Years later, people asked me where Merk ended up, as if men like him go into cold storage until needed. Actually, I heard he worked at his brother's shoe store at Parmatown till he retired to Florida—Lauderdale, I think. I picture him measuring a person's feet with that metal foot-measuring contraption, kneeling in front of strangers and saying, "So, how's 'at in the toe box?" Yep. Merk sold laces to men who didn't know how to tie up their days. He learned the quiet art of return policies. He told one or two customers a story about a trumpet, a kid, and a deejay he once knew. He did not exaggerate. He didn't have to.

Me? Well, let's just say I didn't handle it well, that day when me and radio broke up. We didn't fight over custody or divide the furniture. Radio just walked away from a kid too young to realize you can't divorce something that's already inside your bones.

I went home with the trumpet bumping against my knees like my ol' dog Walter. I slid it under my bed, then pulled it out, then put it back, the way you do with a thought you're not ready to stop thinking about. I ran a finger along the bell again. It made a quiet ring even without air—metal talking to skin. I lifted it and set the mouthpiece where it belonged. I didn't blow into it. I just breathed. The horn smelled like Dicky's jacket and the room I'd worked in at KYW. I stared at that trumpet until the brass blurred. I was twelve, and for the first time, I almost hated the thing I loved.

Downstairs, our copy of *The Press* was on the kitchen table. The headline didn't change when I looked away and looked back. Newsprint rarely has the decency to soften while you aren't watching.

I turned on the table radio, then turned it off, then turned it on again and hated myself for looking to it for comfort. I paced. I tried to read Camus and found that Sisyphus, the damn fool, was still pushing. I went outside and watched a broadcast tower blink against the dusk like a lighthouse for the lost and found. I also knew it was no longer blinking for me.

So, I wrote it a letter that I didn't send. It began: Dear Radio, It wasn't me. It was you that ended it, Goodbye for now. Between those lines, I put nothing, because sometimes nothing is the truest thing. Silence can be a message, too.

You might think a kid can't break up with a thing that doesn't know his name. You'd be wrong. I loved Radioland as if it was a real person. It told me stories, jokes, played me songs, and let me sit under a blanket tent long after my Mom thought I was asleep. It introduced me to a man who handed me a trumpet and a book and the kind of sentence you only understand when you're older: Do something meaningful with your rock. And then, because of a joke about Polish ham cut the wrong way, it shrugged and tossed that man to the street. I couldn't forgive it. Not that day.

That night, I let myself be twelve, which is to say I wept once more, quietly, so my mother wouldn't hear, and whispered to the instrument under my bed as if it could answer.

I went to sleep early with the window cracked open to the Cleveland night. Somewhere, a late bus sighed. Somewhere, a neighbor coughed. Somewhere, the tower blinked. In the morning, I would begin the part of my story where I tried to be just another kid again.

In case you're worried I stayed broken, don't be. I wish I could tell you I'd handled it better. Truth is, I didn't. I did, however, carry that horn with me for years, shoved away, too guilty to throw it out, too heartbroken to play it.

For now, let me leave you with what the paper forgot to print. There was also a boy in a bar with a trumpet in a bag, and Dicky, a man with a bruised mind, was still being kind to him. The rest you can read in headlines. That day, I realized that voices on the air could vanish and that the men behind the mics weren't invincible.

And if you want a moral, you're in the wrong medium. The jingle doesn't cure the day. A slogan won't save the soul. Sometimes all we get is a horn we didn't expect to own, a friend who won't let us drown, and the patience to wait for the next series of odd coincidences that make up a life.

There's a discernible mean streak in living, sure, but it also has a sense of timing. It often waits exactly one beat past your patience and then tosses you a rope. Because what happened next almost made up for it. Not everything, and not forever. Just enough to get me to the next hill with something like a much-needed laugh.

TWELVE — Of Pigs and Princes

"The decline of a great power does not happen in a moment, but in a series of ridiculous scenes."—Anonymous

Rhonda was the first to scream.

The sound crackled through the marble lobby of KYW like microphone feedback. One second, she was perched behind the reception desk, sorting mail with the bored efficiency of a United Auto Worker. The next second, she was scrambling onto the reception desk itself, knees knocking, skirt hiked, eyes wide as saucers.

Why? Because two giant hogs—literal farm-bred hogs—were staring her down.

Not the cute, pink cartoon kind you'd find on a breakfast sausage package, but two living, snorting, stinking brutes, their hooves clattering against the polished lobby floor. Strings of mucus and dung hung from their snouts and, as they grunted forward, the animals tracked dark, runny trails. Pig poop. Real, steaming, and unavoidable.

One porcine intruder wore a sign around its thick neck, letters scrawled in a hand that suggested mischief more than malice: "Ken." The other placard read: "Art."

And so it was, two pigs trotting all over the KYW fortress, branded with the names of the very men who ran the place.

Then Art and his Sansabelt pants arrived. His face puffed up, temple veins pulsing— charging forward as though the building itself had been assaulted. And it had. This wasn't just an invasion of livestock; this was a joke written in pigshit, and everyone knew who the punchline was.

Ken wasn't far behind, his tie swinging loose, his hands flapping at the pigs as if he could herd them like pigeons in the park. It was useless. The hogs were in charge now, snuffling past reception, heading straight toward the elevators as though they had important meetings on the top floor.

Rhonda shrieked again, clutching a pencil cup like it was full of holy water. Around them, sales assistants, engineers, even Mr. Plant, the janitor, with his mop bucket—scattering, slipping, falling, hollering. You'd think a shit bomb had gone off. Well, two bombs in pig form.

I never found out exactly how Merk pulled it off. Who else would have the guts, or the gall, or the contacts willing to lend him livestock for a prank of biblical proportions? It had all his fingerprints: crude humor, a jab at authority, and just enough chaos to make Art look like a buffoon.

Art's face boiled red as he flung his arms toward the swine. "Get them out! For Christ's sake, somebody GET THEM OUT!"

But nobody did. The pigs were having the time of their lives. One rooted its snout under a chair, flipping it over with a triumphant grunt. The other slipped on its own mess, squealed, and barreled straight into a magazine rack. Flyers for the local auto show scattered into the air like confetti at a parade.

And through it all, those signs swung back and forth: Ken. Art. Ken. Art. Like little cardboard marquees of shame.

I swear, if you'd been there, you'd have thought the universe itself had decided to stage a protest against KYW. Years of slick promotion, polished brass plaques, and earnest civic awards— undone in a heartbeat by two hogs with indigestion. The giant pigs munched on chair cushions and shoved around leather couches like they were demonic employees of Old McDonald's Movers.

Rhonda, still trembling atop her desk, wailed, "Do something!"

Ken lunged at the pig wearing his name tag, arms out, only to skid in a shit puddle and land flat on his backside. One hog snorted directly at his face and almost smiled.

Art wasn't faring much better. He jabbed at the "Art" designated hog with a rolled-up magazine, but the beast ripped the periodical from his hand, almost biting through his thumb. When riled and afraid, sows are mean and have sharper teeth than anyone can imagine! Giant, prize-winning hogs are many things: smart as a dog, a cat, or even a three-year-old human child, but very aggressive when hungry, and even domesticated pigs often attack their owners.

Well, these two proud porkies were both voracious eaters, and I'm guessing Merk made sure they hadn't had their breakfast. These girls were ready to consume almost anything they got their snouts on!

The lobby had become a barnyard, the high-gloss veneer stripped away to reveal something primal and absurd.

And me? I got a really early phone call from Merk asking me to meet him outside the front window of the station at 9:30 a.m. to watch this strange mix of horror and delight. Art saw us standing outside. For me, it was worth skipping school for a half-day to see the show.

"KEAGELS! YOU NO GOOD SONOFABITCH!" Art's voice exploded across the lobby.

Merk just laughed, "The bastid told me he'd put pig shit on KYW. Hey, I'm jus' helpin' the fucker out!"

I knew I was witnessing the end of something—though whether it was the end of KYW's dignity or the start of the "Legend of Merk: The Prankster Prince," I couldn't quite tell.

All around, people yelled and scrambled, but there was no corralling them. The pigs had won. They owned the space. The adverts on their necks said it all: Ken and Art, reduced to swine. After a few minutes, we walked off laughing so hard we almost pissed ourselves, but the mayhem went on for a while until a tight-lipped (and very well-paid) farmer pulled up with a trailer and ushered the stinky intruders home for their actual morning repast.

When I think back now, older, grayer, with my own share of indignities, it all feels fitting. Empires don't collapse with solemn speeches or marble statues crumbling in the rain. They go out with farce. They go out with a squeal and a shit puddle on the lobby floor.

And KYW, my first true cathedral of sound, was no different.

Not long after that, many other good KYW Radio people got fired, too. Engineers who maintained two giant alternating transmitters: Phil, Jerry G.'s board operator, who always wore Hawaiian shirts; Chick was out, too, as was a copywriter who always wore a heavy cardigan because Art's nearby air conditioner was too ambitious. Good people. The kind who made you a sandwich when you were too polite to ask. They didn't have enemies; they had lives, kids, and mortgages. But still, the day came when someone from upstairs—someone new to the station's ghosts—handed them a white envelope and a speech about "different directions." Then, their station keys no longer fit the new locks. I learned that a place can love you at 9:05 and kick your butt out by lunch.

Back at home, Walter, my always-faithful pup, knew when the day had outlived its usefulness. By nightfall, he'd nuzzle my knee, a polite reminder that even a boy needs a place to hide. We built it together—blankets fastened to the bedposts, draped in slack arcs that turned my room into a small red cave, and my transistor radio was its hearth. Walter sniffed it with suspicion, then dropped his head on his paws like a sentry after his shift.

Walter snored softly. I thumbed the dial in careful half-moons, the way Alvy once showed me—"Never jerk the dial, Tom-bo, jus' nudge it." On a good night, I could bounce around the Midwest on a wire made of air: 1120/KMOX, St. Louis, reading off the rising Mississippi River flood stages; "The Big 8"/CKLW, Detroit, sounding like it had too many cars and not enough sidewalks; a polite Canadian voice on 1050/CHUM discussing weather that required a Mounted Police's courage to face; and 700/WLW, "The Voice of the Cincinnati Reds!"—the only station in America that was once permitted to broadcast at 500,000 watts. I'm told if you held two metal objects together, you could actually hear the station's signal vibrating! But home was the sound I longed for, and KYW's new "voice" just wasn't the same. It seemed shy of itself.

Suddenly, it was the summer of '65, and one morning, I heard a rumor that KYW was about to change uniforms. I biked down Euclid because my legs needed evidence. The station's lobby looked as it always had—Rhonda still on duty, the ficus chastened after its run-in with the pigs. But outside, on the building's limestone façade, some men arrived with ladders—workmen with the faces of good intentions and overtime dreams. Their truck doors thunked closed with an authority that makes you step aside without being told.

New signage went up. One guy climbing, one below footing the ladder, a third handing up a pry bar. The first letter came away with a soft wrenching sound, the way old gum loosens from the underside of a pew. Then off came the Y, then W. And with each, I felt that tiny pang in my chest again.

They wrapped the letters in a moving blanket and carried them off like Mafia murder victims. Empty screw holes became bullet marks left on the building.

"Hold it steady," someone said.

"Watch your left."

A new crate opened. Shiny letters—barely touched by human hands—were handed up the ladder like commandments ascending the wrong mountain. W... K... Y... C. It looked familiar if you squinted—the way a person does after a bad haircut.

The owner's plate below changed, too. The line of lineage was rewritten with a drill and a rivet gun: WKYC, National Broadcasting Company.

The men stepped back, wiped brick dust from their palms, and crooked their heads at their own handiwork. They had no quarrel with either name. They were paid to attach nouns and consonants to stone. But for me, grammar matters!

Yep. K-Y-W/Cleveland was gone. It had packed up and moved to Philly.

The strange change had both the weight of a benediction and the thud of a closing door. We'd traded one set of letters for another and sent our old call sign to a different skyline—KYW would now speak "All News, All the Time" from a city I'd only visited in baseball box scores.

The new on-air jingles arrived next, of course—much shorter, more strategic, focused mostly on station identification, and light as helium with female-led vocals, not the giant choir I was used to.

"W-K-Y-C... Fun-nun-nun!" they sang.

If you heard it in a vacuum, you'd think "cheerful" had been invented by radio jingles. But the first thing you learn in Radioland is that joy and marketing often share the same tailor. The jingle trilled from the outside lobby speaker, bounced off the marble and Rhonda's lacquered hair, and came back to me thinner, as if it had lost some calories in the echoes.

Inside, management had a small laugh for anyone still invested: "Same station, just more music!" They didn't say "minus heart," not because they were liars but because hearts weren't on their spreadsheets. The workmen packed up the old letters and drove away without ceremony. Somewhere, a storeroom would cradle K, Y, W in the dark like relics or most likely be tossed away.

That night, I folded myself back into the blanket tent, like a moth seeking its old lamp. The radio warmed my ear. Walter breathed his eloquent dog breath across the speaker, and signals combed the room.

I tried to take the jingle's advice. "Fun-nun-nun"? Really? Nope.

I even said the new call sign out loud to see if the syllables made any sense. They didn't. "W-K-Y-C"? Hmpf. At least the new calls still had a K and a Y—so joy was not a consonant and vowel problem.

People will tell you places don't die, they just change names. Those people have never stood on a sidewalk watching a set of letters pulled out like teeth from a giant's mouth.

Rhonda would tell the story of the hogs for another decade, her voice always landing on the same note when she remembered the way the pig looked at her—like it knew her salary. Ken would tell his own story, leaving out the pigs—about steering a station through a "transition," about his "vision," and "strategy," and blah, blah, blah. Merk, if you caught him in the right mood and bought him the right whiskey, would laugh and say: "You shoulda seen the grins on 'em fuckin' pigs."

I had my own version: a boy under a blanket, unwilling to forgive, and his dog that forgave everything.

The new WKYC's on-air booth was now a combo operation—management's proud phrase for "one jock does everything." No board-op at the helm, no Chick catching a cue while the jock riffed. Instead, the deejay himself was expected to juggle it all: patter, buttons, records, jingles, and commercial logs. It was cheap efficiency dressed up as innovation. One fewer person meant one fewer salary and no health insurance obligations.

And into that new, sterile cockpit, they dropped their bright young hope: a kid they christened "the fastest talker in radio." He looked barely out of school, a mop of hair fluffed with no part, sideburns cut with a straightedge. He leaned into the mic with the bravado of a carnival barker and let it rip.

"WOO! It's Big Jack, your LEE-dah, honey!" His words flew out like buckshot, barely separated, each one tripping over the next. "Aw, it's a blue Monday, babies, cuz school's back in at Lorraine High!"

I imagined Lorraine High groaning in unison, kids in pressed button-downs dragging their feet while Big Jack turned their yield to history class into a jingle. And then, without missing a beat, Jack shifted his voice into something altogether different: a raspy, close-mic growl. "And don't forget ME! Your naked nighttime Neanderthal: Gorilla-man!"

Yep, "Big" Jackson Armstrong had invented a sidekick out of thin air, a gorilla who rasped, chortled, and gave the illusion of a duet. The trick impressed some, but I could almost hear Chick's ghost sigh from studio control. In Dicky's day, a single trumpet honk could carry the weight of a thousand gimmicks. Big Jack needed an imaginary ape to get through his shift. (I know, they were all gimmicks, Dicky's too. But shut up! I was pissed and thought being mean felt appropriate!)

He slapped a button, cueing the next song with the care of a man swatting flies. The jingle singers burst through the airwaves, syrupy and insistent: "W-K-Y-C, Radio 11! Super Hit Three! (Hit Three! Hit Three!")

And then came the Rolling Stones, guitars snarling as "Satisfaction" clawed its way into the booth. Mick Jagger's voice stretched through the speakers like elastic, and for a moment, I thought the room might come alive again. But it wasn't Dicky's chaos, not even close. It was a record dropped in on cue, neat as a tax form.

From my blanket fort, Walter curled up at my feet. I listened critically. Big Jack really did talk fast—so fast it was hard to catch the gaps where a thought might breathe. And that was the trick, wasn't it? Fill the hour with fast chatter, squeeze in shorter jingles, and wedge more commercials between the music's hooks. Speed wasn't energy; it was smokescreen. The faster things went, the more commercials they played, and the more a station could bill.

I missed the mess. Dicky's sweat, his dangerous grin, his jokes that landed sideways and threatened to topple into disaster, but saving a dud bit was Dicky's real talent. His crazy ad libs made to save bad situations were his gift—that was the radio I loved. To me, Big Jack was just a stopwatch.

And, in my now thirteen-year-old gut, I knew this wasn't Radioland anymore. This was Salesland with a soundtrack. But, then, it always was, wasn't it?

The Stones fizzled out, Big Jack's gorilla growled, and I shut the transistor off with a snap. The silence that followed had weight. Walter sighed, rolled to his side, and thumped his tail once, as if to remind me that dogs don't need radios; they already understand the world.

I crawled deeper into the blanket fort, the fabric sagging over me like the roof of some private chapel. The transistor sat in the middle like a relic. I sighed, clicked it back on, and spun the dial—not to find WKYC, but to lose myself in anything else.

The static came first, a hiss stretched across an electronic desert. Then, faint voices bled in and out: a weather forecast from 1520/WKBW, Buffalo, far too polite for Cleveland's frozen ears. A farm report from 1190/WOWO, Indiana, talking soybeans like they were scripture. Each station flared, vanished, and faded in heterodyne distortion. I realized that the air was crowded with voices, all of them battling to be heard.

As the dial skipped, I also realized this was what love really sounded like when it ended. Not with a bang, not with a speech, not even with two pigs defiling a marble lobby. It ended in clutter. Too many voices, too much noise, none of them the one you wanted.

There it was, the confession, soft as a dog's snore. Radio had been my first romance, my first idol, my first heartbreak. Dicky was gone, the call letters were gone, even Merk had vanished into some shoe store life. But in that moment, inside the sagging cathedral of my blanket tent, I realized I'd carry the hum forever.

Walter pressed his cold nose against my arm, grounding me, reminding me that silence wasn't empty. It was alive and waiting. I rubbed his velvet ears, tuned one more notch to nowhere, and whispered to myself: Hubba-hubba.

So, that's it. The story of my first big love affair. And it all happened way back when… in Radioland.

Thirteen — The Corps of the Story

"We do not remember days, we remember moments."—Cesare Pavese

T he first thing you notice when you step into National Public Radio's StoryCorps trailer is how quiet it is. Inside the roomy, rolling Airstream, all outside noise dissolves. The world pares itself down to your own breath, the shuffle of your clothes, and the tick of your throat when you swallow. The NPR engineers turned this retrofitted silver bullet into a sanctuary for memory—a place where ordinary people sit across from a microphone and suddenly, somehow, sound like prophets.

I wasn't sure I belonged there. At seventy-something, with a beard gone to milk and knees like bad shocks on a used car, I didn't feel like a prophet. But when I heard the StoryCorps van was rolling into Cleveland's NPR station, I knew this was something I had to get off my chest. Something I'd been thinking about and carrying with me for more than six decades. Maybe, if I could just tell the story out loud, I could finally put it to rest.

The booth smelled faintly of carpet glue and coffee. A young woman—efficient, invisible in the way people are when they've been trained to vanish behind glass—gave me a pleasant smile through the control room window. She clicked a switch. A red light blinked. My story, she said, would now become part of the legacy of StoryCorps and would be placed in the Library of Congress.

I leaned toward the mic, my voice roughened by years of pipe smoking.

"Funny," I began, and the word felt both too small and too right. "It was really only a few months in a kid's life, but, aw, I dunno. I can't seem to let it go. I... still dream about her. Still... haunted by the... voices."

I hadn't planned to say it like that. But that's what StoryCorps does—it strips away the years until you're twelve again, heart bruised, trying to explain why radio waves at one short time in my life felt like the breath of God.

There was a pause, the kind where silence isn't empty but expectant. Then the intercom clicked. The producer's voice filtered through, careful but curious. "Just tell us all about it in your own words," she said.

I nodded slowly and began. And I just... talked, and talked, and talked, it seemed like for hours, and I told the entire story, the one you just read—as honestly as I could remember it. And the young woman in the booth listened, never interrupting, never stopping me until she asked, "So, did you... ever get into broadcasting, Doctor Bianco?"

I barked a laugh—half scoff, half sigh. "Me? Nah. I was never really built for radio. Kept my promise, though." Then involuntarily, I patted my heart. "Did thirty-three years at Cleveland Clinic. Neurological and psychiatric disorders. Yeah, I, I'd like to think... um... I helped a lot of... good people."

I said it like I believed it, and on most days, I do. But the kid under the blanket fort would've rolled his eyes. The woman in the booth hesitated, then leaned toward the mic. "And Dicky? Whatever happened to him?"

The name landed like a stone deep in my gut. For a second, I thought the walls of the Airstream might shiver with it.

I looked down at my hands—veined, aged with small spots, shaking slightly. What could I possibly tell her? That Dicky was the sun and the burn at the same time? That he made me laugh until my stomach ached and then made me stare into the abyss before my voice had cracked? That he was as much illness as genius?

Instead, I cleared my throat. "Yeah, um... you might wanna stop the recording on this part, dear." I leaned in, lowered my voice. "That is, I mean... if you don't mind."

Through the glass, I saw her eyebrows lift. She was young, polite, the kind who still believed technology obeys human decency.

"Oh? Oh, sure."

Her finger tapped a button. I heard the click of the stop. But my voice still trembled in the headphones. The waveform still danced across her monitor in her glasses. Just a trick of habit, I suppose. Recordists never really stop when someone says, "off the record." They just pretend.

She gave me a small nod—half professional, half complicit. I could see it in her eyes: she wanted the story, and she'd let me tell it my way.

"Look," I said, and the word scraped against my throat. "Dick was a... tortured guy. Cyclothymic, delusional, hallucinating. Seesawed between... mania and madness." A pause, a revelation, then I continued. "Yeah, Dicky... was radio."

I let the words hang. Because they were the truest thing I could ever say about him.

"So, a few days before he was supposed to head up to his new gig in Detroit, he drives out to, ah... to Edgewater Park..."

And then a film rolled in my mind.

The car creaked as it pulled to a stop on the sandlot, the Cleveland skyline cut in jagged shapes against the late afternoon sky. Inside, the air smelled of bourbon and hopelessness. Dicky tilted the bottle back, his throat working like a man trying to drown himself. Then lit up a smoke, cigarette ash dropping onto his shirt.

Beside him, in the passenger seat, sat the Faceless Black Manikin again. Of course, it wasn't really there. But in Dicky's world, it always had a ticket. In its outstretched hand, a book: Resistance, Rebellion, and Death, Albert Camus. The Frenchman who gave him existentialist answers—ones that only prompted deeper questions about human suffering.

Dicky reached for it, fingers trembling. He swigged bourbon, then opened the pages. His lips moved silently over the words. His chest heaved. He lit another cigarette, then another. Tears streaked down his cheeks, carving tiny rivers into the mask of sweat.

Eventually, the bottle rolled empty against the passenger seat. The book slipped from his lap to the floor. And his lit cigarette fell with it.

Fire moves faster than grief. The book caught first, then accelerated by the whiskey, then the seat. The flames roared like an audience demanding more, and Dicky, slumped over the wheel, barely stirred.

The car became a furnace, then an explosion. For one wild second, it seemed to leap off the ground, as if trying to take flight toward the skyline it could never reach.

And… it was over.

His body lay at the Cuyahoga County Medical Examiner's Office, unclaimed, until his mother identified the body nearly two weeks later.

"My God," the young woman whispered through the glass.

I rubbed my eyes, pretending dust had gotten in. "So, ah… it might be best to stop with the pig shit story," I said, forcing a smile. "It'll give you… y'know, a fun… radio ending."

Her lips parted as though to argue, but she thought better of it. She nodded, professional again, though her face had softened.

And that was that. The official story ended with pigs in the lobby, a punchline on eight hooves. The rest — Dicky's inferno, my own haunted dreams—belonged to me. Or maybe to no one. I didn't argue against using it. That was none of my business. StoryCorps would decide.

The red light blinked off. The intercom clicked silent. She opened the door and ushered me out. My shoes clanged as I walked cautiously down the metal steps.

The Cleveland sky had cleared, blue as a postcard, gulls carving lazy arcs above the lot. I shook hands, offered polite thanks, and walked toward the only car waiting in the rarely-seen Cleveland sun.

Epilogue —

"What we have once enjoyed we can never lose. All that we love deeply becomes a part of us."—Helen Keller

The car hummed low as I steered it northwest. At my age, every drive feels like a pilgrimage—the scrape of tires, the drone of the motor, and the way the road pulls you forward as if on autopilot. I'd been telling stories all morning, my voice trapped in digital amber inside that silver NPR Airstream, and now I craved silence.

On the seat beside me sat the object I hadn't touched in years: Dicky's battered trumpet. The valves tarnished from neglect. It still smelled faintly of cigarette smoke.

I pulled off at one of the lonely overlooks near Lake Erie. The lot was empty, just a wide sweep of asphalt and the lake beyond, stretching blue and endless. On the radio, Sinatra sang "That Old Black Magic." I clicked it off. I've had more than enough magic for one lifetime. I killed the engine, and for a moment, I let the car sit in the hush, the trumpet glinting in dappled light.

I lifted the horn, felt its surprising weight, and stepped out into the air.

The path down to the beach was no path at all—just a steep embankment of sand and stubborn dune grass. I half-slid, half-stumbled my way down, old bones cursing, shoes filling with grit. At the bottom, the lake greeted me, restless but not unfriendly. Waves slapped the shore like a hand tapping to remind you it's still there.

I raised the trumpet, pressed the cool metal to my lips, and blew. The sound was a honk more than a note, raw and comic. Still, it carried.

"Hubba-hubba!" I shouted after it, cupping my hand to my mouth like the kid I once was. The dunes threw the words back at me in crooked echoes. I laughed, the kind of laugh that hurts a little. For a second, I listened, half-expecting Dicky to answer.

I settled on a rock, my tobacco pipe in hand, and lit it against the lake breeze. Smoke curled up, white and thin, vanishing before it could form anything solid. I grabbed at it like a boy again, trying to hold onto a dissolving ghost, but it slipped away. As everything does.

Funny how something so brief can imprint, can brand you for life. Only a few months in a radio booth, scribbling names, sneaking peeks, learning patter, falling deeper in love—and here I am, decades later, still measuring the world against those nights.

What did it say in that Shakespeare play? The one my wife and I saw that time? I muttered to myself: "I am lulled into meaning. And that is the greatest fiction of all." I wasn't sure if I had it right, but it felt close enough.

I reached into my jacket and pulled out the old Polaroid, edges brown and curling. There we were again: me, Alvy with his twitching hands, and Dicky, distracted even in the split second of the shutter. Three ghosts trapped forever in a square of fading chemicals.

There's a song that says every kid's wish will be heard and answered. Beautiful poetry, that. I prayed for radio, for its signal to never fade, for Dicky to keep honking his trumpet forever. And like all childish prayers, it was madness. But it was mine.

I closed my eyes, and the flashbacks came—not as memories but like eight-millimeter film reels unspooling.

Alvy and me outside the KYW building, me pledging my allegiance to a jingle that had long since been erased. Noses pressed to the glass like hungry orphans. Alvy using stubby fingers to find what hid behind a reluctant zipper in the KYW men's room. Then his face, forlorn, in the window of the bus pulling away, tears streaking as he mouthed words I couldn't hear. A heartbreak that still eats at me—an apology that never came. Just images that flashed in staccato.

And then came Walter! When I looked up, I saw my sweet ol' dog, Walt—such a good boy—bounding across the sand like he'd been waiting for me all this time. I swear I saw him—really saw him—ears flying, tongue lolling, barking with joy. I bent down, arms open, but he faded before I could feel him again. My chest ached in the exact shape of his absence. Ah, the mind plays tricks.

I turned back to the water, blinking hard. The Lady in the Lake was peaceful that day. She had been rolling against this shore eons before me, before Dicky, before radio towers stabbed the sky. She would keep rolling for eons after.

And Dicky's words came back, too—that night in the booth, his eyes bloodshot and his voice low. It's all... pointless, Tommy.

Maybe he was right. Maybe the pig pranks, the jingles, the long nights of patter, were just momentary static written on the wind.

I shook my head, pipe smoke stinging my eyes. "Too bad, Dicky," I said softly. "Because you and all of it—every second—sure meant something to me."

That's the paradox, isn't it? Pointless, sure. But making it mean something, in the end, is our great work on this Earth, and all we really have.

I let the words settle in my mind, then stood. My knees popped in protest. The trumpet sat on the rock beside me, silent, its bell catching a flicker of sun. I reached for it, then stopped. I didn't need to carry it anymore. Some burdens you honor by leaving them behind.

I smiled—not sad, not happy, just… knowing. The gulls cried overhead. The day was perfect… Absurdly perfect, as the lake stretched past my vision.

As I walked back to the car, I said out loud to no one in particular, "And that…

Just then, another sharp, sudden memory popped, blinding in its brightness. It came from that first day in the KYW production room when Merk tousled Alvy's hair and shrugged:

"That's showbiz, kids."

It stopped me in my tracks… and I smiled, for real this time, nodded, and just kept moving forward.

If anyone had been there, they might have heard me humming a scrap of melody by the Beatles—the group that had once been banned in Cleveland, now free… and gone.

"In my life, I loved you more…" —Lennon/McCartney, 1965.

Radioland is a fictional tale, but the disease from which the story's Dicky Peppers suffers is very real. Call it what you will: depression, mania, bipolar disorder, schizophrenia, or despair, there are professionals in your area ready to help.

If you or someone you love is agonized by a debilitating mental challenge, assistance is always available. Anyone, at any age, who is experiencing a suicidal and/or substance use crisis may call, text, or chat 24/7. It's free and confidential.

Or you might text: 988. That's the Suicide & Crisis Lifeline, ready 24/7 at no obligation to you.

You can also text: HOME to 741741 to reach a trained crisis counselor through the Crisis Text Line, a global not-for-profit organization. It's also free, confidential, and always available, day or night. For online help, tap in: 988lifeline.org

Skilled, judgment-free counselors are waiting to provide real and compassionate support. You deserve to feel heard and cared for, anytime, anywhere, 24/7/365.

Why wait, right?

Acknowledgments —

To the countless radio voices of my youth, especially the on-air personalities—the pranksters, jokesters, and poets of the airwaves—thank you for filling the nights with laughter, music, and possibilities. Thanks, too, to anyone who ever slipped a tiny transistor radio under a pillow and fell asleep to those faceless voices they loved way back when. This one's for you.

My gratitude extends to my brother, Dr. Albert M. Pondillo, Ph.D., clinical psychologist, who guided me through the dark corridors of the bipolar mind. Al's insights into the behaviors of the mentally ill and how each manic episode manifests the pain of depression opened my eyes and heart. Thanks, bro.

A big "thankyouandyourewelcome" to my oldest and dearest friend, David H. Lawrence XVII, my brother from another cliché, and the narrator of the audiobook version of this work. David was always ready to assist with excellent notes, savvy observations, and (often hilarious) counsel. It's a blessing to have a long-term buddy who has witnessed multiple versions of me, yet can still say he loves me.

Oh, and a very special thanks to my pal and former colleague in the college professorin' biz, Dick Taylor, consultant, entrepreneur, self-acknowledged "radio guy" and one outstanding blogger (https://dicktaylorblog.com/tag/hd-radio/). He was the first to recommend, "You should write a book!" So please, blame Dick.

Finally, to my early readers: Mike Olszewski, Jon Belmont, Eric Braun, Mary Hood Hart, Frank Robertson, Chris Stager, Drew Carey, Dr. Jim Hoyt, Dale "The Voice-Man" Reeves, KYW's Jay Lawrence, Dave McBride, Emily and Luke DeAndrade, Matthew Lickel, Mac Currie, Shelby Lackey, Peggy Murphy, Jon and Judy Urness, Suzanne Goodyear-Pondillo, Dan Haber, Dr. Jerod Ra'Del Hollyfield, Karen Luedtke Moore Josephson, Jim Davison, Dr. Bob Spires, Dr. Mary Nichols, cartoon VO talent Greg Berg, "Dean of Detroit

Radio" Kevin O'Neill, the brilliant actor and voice talent Ed Kelly, and of course, "Radio's Best Friend" Art Vuolo.

Thanks a million for the gift of your time.

About the Author —

Bob Pondillo is a multi-award-winning short filmmaker, writer/director, and taught beginning and advanced Screenplay Writing, Media History, and related media and culture classes at the College of Media and Entertainment at Middle Tennessee State University, where he was a tenured, full-time faculty member for fourteen years.

His short narrative movies, *Would You Cry If I Died?* (2006), *My Name Is Wallace* (2007), *Wait...* (2008), and *The New, True, Charlie Wu* (2010) have won dozens of awards from film festivals around the nation and the world, including "Best Screenplay," "Best Director" and more than 30 "Best of Fest" honors. Both *My Name Is Wallace* and *Wait...* were chosen as "Official Selections" in more than 100 film festivals, including the prestigious Festival de Cannes, Cannes, France, in 2007 and 2008. His short narrative film, *The Miracles on Honey Bee Hill*, a story about forgiveness, love, and acceptance, won more than 30 film festivals around the globe and was even translated into Czech for the Mezipatria Film Festival in Prague. His sixth short film project, *Happy New Year, Mr. Kates!* garnered "Best Screenplay 2012" honors from the prestigious American International Film Festival, Chicago, and was awarded the Audience Choice Award: Best Film/2014 from Nashville's ARTLightenment Film Festival. All of his short films are available on YouTube.

Pondillo worked in the media industry—radio/TV and film—before coming to academia. His credits include The Voice of America, Washington, D.C.; WNBC Radio, New York; ABC Radio Networks, New York; Group W Productions, Los Angeles; Paramount Pictures Television, Los Angeles; as well as more than 20 local radio and television stations from Ohio to Florida. He created the Emmy Award-winning Cleveland Comedy Company, co-founded and acted as Creative Director for the syndicated American Comedy Network, and in 2002 was inducted into the Radio/Television Broadcasters Hall of Fame in Akron, Ohio.

Dr. Robert J. Pondillo earned his Ph.D. from the University of Wisconsin-Madison and holds the title of Emeritus Professor of Media/Culture, and Screenwriting. In addition to his numerous scholarly publications on media history and culture, Pondillo has written two academic books: *America's First Network TV Censor: The Work of NBC's Stockton Helffrich* (Southern Illinois University Press, 2010), and *American Media and Social Institutions* (Cognella, 2014.) Radioland is his first novel, adapted from his original full-length motion picture screenplay of the same title.

He lives with his wife in Madison, Wisconsin, where he often still mourns his first dog, sweet old Walter.

KYW—

Radioland is a work of fiction, a flight of fancy wrapped around some actual facts. For example, radio station KYW, the station at which the story is set, really did move from Cleveland to Philadelphia on June 19, 1965, by order of the U.S. Department of Justice and the Federal Communications Commission. This occurred after a call letter "swap" with the Westinghouse Electric & Manufacturing Company (through its broadcast subsidiary, Group W) and the National Broadcasting Company (NBC).

Actual KYW history reveals that, from the early through the mid-twentieth century, those grand old call letters had always had a bit of a bumpy ride. KYW radio first began broadcasting in 1921 Chicago, where they often changed frequencies from 560 khz to 1020 khz, then back down to 570 khz and back up to 1020 khz. Later came the stations' ownership "swaps" from Westinghouse to NBC then back to Westinghouse.

This effort sparked a protracted legal tussle, some of it most unsavory. Among the reasons for all this "jockeying for position" included a rapidly changing technology that brought the arrival of more competition, a growing and younger popular culture, and radio's hunt for specific new audiences to serve. Such changes also welcomed the then-novel strategy that stations could pinpoint programming to narrow sets of demographics to generate more ad revenue. Arguably, the key factor for the switch was the eventual government-mandated decision that put an end to the long and often ferocious legal battle.

KYW only stayed in Cleveland for nine years, from 1956-65, but carved out an indelible identity that many remember to this day.

Now, as a writer of historical fiction, I recognize the above as an example of how manic radio was and how rapidly it could change. I noticed how such behaviors meshed well with the human themes of my story—birth, growth, change, loss, and rebirth. Within those universal

311

conditions—in both business and life—we learn, grow, change, experience hurt, and grow anew.

But the above is just the tip of the true KYW story. Should you be interested, I invite you to read retired Cleveland State University Professor Dr. Richard Klein's brilliant history of the station. You can download it here: "KYW Radio: The Cleveland Years" by Richard Klein. It's a fascinating read and a truly outstanding publication.

Finally, for those who've asked, "Was there ever really a "Swingin' Dicky Peppers?" No. I modeled Dicky's character and some of the grim details of his death, after an actual radio personality. His name was Barney Pip. As a kid, I would listen to him at night on "Big 10"/WCFL-AM, Chicago. I never met Barney, but like Tommy in the story, I grew to love him. If you'd like to hear his voice and radio persona, just Google: Barney Pip/WCFL.

I'm grateful to deejay Richard "Ricky" Kaufman, who knew Barney as a mentor and good friend. Ricky and I spent many hours together reminiscing about the old days. Thanks, then, to "Ricky the K" and his "Solid Gold Time Machine" heard in the '90s on 1520/KOMA, "Oklahoma's Most Listened-to Oldies Station." Through Ricky, I came to better understand and even more admire the courage of the late Barney Pip.

Final Shameless Plug:

If you're inclined to learn more about Cleveland radio and TV—officially designated the "Rock and Roll Capital of the World" in 1972—check out the many books written by my friend, media historian Mike Olszewski. Mike's got an entire library waiting for you! Google him at: Amazon, Barnes & Noble, Books-a-MIllion and wherever online books are sold.

By the way, I had the great pleasure of adapting one of Mike's nonfiction books—*Mad Daddy: Myers, Mintz and the Moondog* and *How Cleveland, Ohio Changed Rock Radio*—to a fictionalized full-length motion picture screenplay. Mad Daddy is another dynamite Olszewski work and, of course, one terrific read.

www.ingramcontent.com/pod-product-compliance
Lightning Source LLC
Chambersburg PA
CBHW071246170626
46809CB00001B/99